Valerons - Beyond the Law!

It sounded simple enough – Wyatt Valeron is hired to escort a man from Paradise to Denver, Colorado. However, upon arrival at the secluded mining town, he learns a sinister tyrant named Gaskell controls everyone and everything. His hired 'enforcers' maintain a form of law that supersedes all outside authority. To break a rule can mean punishment or even death. Wyatt does what comes naturally and ends up sentenced to hang.

With the Valerons going into action to save Wyatt and take on the all-powerful men in Paradise, another problem has landed on the family doorstep. Cliff Mason finds himself drawn to the plight of a runaway girl, a girl with a dark secret and terrible fear of the man searching for her.

Both dilemmas have a similar challenge – the authorities are unable to do anything without proof. The Valerons must act on their own to stop these criminals who are Beyond the Law.

Valerons - Beyond the Law!

Terrell L. Bowers

A Black Horse Western

ROBERT HALE

© Terrell L. Bowers 2019
First published in Great Britain 2019

ISBN 978-0-7198-2888-1

The Crowood Press
The Stable Block
Crowood Lane
Ramsbury
Marlborough
Wiltshire SN8 2HR

www.bhwesterns.com

Robert Hale is an imprint
of The Crowood Press

CHAPTER ONE

Wyatt Valeron had never heard of Paradise, Colorado. It was not on regular routes or most of the maps he had seen. The reason, he learned, was due to it not actually being a town, but a corporation. It was a mining conglomerate that had built its own private settlement. He rode into town and discovered there were stores, a bakery, tavern, saloon, and a large hotel with a poster by the front door that boasted amenities usually found only in larger cities. The dozen or so houses in the area were expensive in size and structure, while the numerous barracks-style buildings, all of them two stories high, ran for more than an average city block on either side of the street. Beyond those housing units, there were old railroad boxcars with crude shuttered windows. He surmised there must have been at least twenty or more of those. Having seen a few being used for housing, he suspected that was the case here. The railroad spur did come as far as Paradise, but it went no further than a dock for loading ore. Those cars had been dragged into place, likely by several teams of horses, to serve the need for more housing.

Wyatt stopped at a blacksmith shop, which was also the town livery stable. The man working there stopped what he was doing and came over to greet him.

'Howdy!' Wyatt spoke to him. 'You people are a far piece off of the main trails.'

The man was close to Wyatt's own age, no more than thirty. When he spoke, he had a distinctive accent.

'Yah, we don' get so many travelers up here.'

'Name is Wyatt.'

'Bing,' the man returned.

'Is this a mining town, Bing?'

'Yah, it be dat.' He looked over his ride. 'Nice lookin' mare.'

'I need to put her up for a night or two,' Wyatt said. 'I imagine there are vacancies at the hotel for a room?'

'Dere usually be some. Best service you find anywhere.'

'Is that so?'

'Paradise be no ordinary town; it be a business enterprise.'

Wyatt nodded. 'A fellow in Denver told me it was a corporation.'

'It be a private corporation. No one tell Gaskell how to run his business, I tell you. He be der only law in Paradise.'

'I'll remember.' He paused to look back along the main street. 'Do they have a telegraph office? I saw poles and a wire on my way up from the main road.'

'Yah. It be at the shipping office, next to dah jail.'

'Jail? You have a sheriff or marshal here?' Wyatt asked.

'No, we done got Enforcers; dey wear badges like lawmen. Take care not to cross one of dem.'

'I'm a peaceful sort,' Wyatt told him. Then he handed

6

the man the reins to his horse. 'I'll let you know how many nights, soon as I make contact with my employer.'

'Don' be sending nuthen over der wire what you don' want passed along to Gaskell. He knows everything dat goes on in Paradise.'

Wyatt grinned. 'Like I said, I don't go out of my way to cause trouble. I was hired for a rather simple chore.'

Bing took the horse and led her towards the barn. Wyatt rotated about and started up the street. The cleanliness was far and away above any he had seen. Every building had a fresh coat of stain, there was a solid walkway along both sides of the street, and not a piece of litter to be seen. Each sign on a storefront was neatly posted and every window facing the street appeared spotless. Even as he wondered how they kept it so pristine, a young boy and girl were working diligently, cleaning the windows of the bakery. After a few steps, he saw another girl, not yet in her teens, sweeping the walkway.

Wyatt entered the freight office and was greeted by a heavy-set gent, who had been perched on a stool behind a counter.

'Good day to you, sir. What can I do for you?'

'A fellow named Clevis Mackavoy sent me a wire to meet him here in Paradise. I don't suppose you have a cable for me? Name's Wyatt.'

The man frowned. 'Mackavoy, you say?' At Wyatt's head bob, he rubbed the stubble on his fuzzy chin. 'Young Shelly Mackavoy works at the eatery. Her brother cleans the saloon nights, but I've not seen nor heard of Clevis.'

'He is probably on his way here. It took some looking to find your settlement.'

'Everything you see here is part of the Paradise Land and Mining Corporation.'

'Impressive,' Wyatt said. 'Even the stores and shops?'

'Every house, shop and worker within a mile in any direction,' the man answered.

'Must be taking out a lot of ore.'

'Enough to fill a dozen rail cars each and every week.'

'So you take script for payment here?'

'No, only cash money or on account. The hired and contract workers all have an account number. Anything they want or need is put on their account. If they exceed their monthly allotment, it means having added time to their contract.'

Wyatt did not hide his surprise. 'So most everyone working in this town is indentured in some way?'

'Not indentured. Contracts,' he stated simply. 'I work for wages, as do most of the store and business proprietors,' the man explained. 'We all have workers assigned to help us run and operate our businesses.' He shrugged. 'Some are contract workers and some are convicts too – debtors and those who committed non-violent crimes. Mr Gaskell has agreements with the state and county to employ those workers. So long as the mine is turning a profit, we stay in business.'

Wyatt frowned. 'Without actual indentures, how does Gaskell get so many contract workers?'

'Still a lot of people who want to come to America that can't afford the passage. They sign a contract to work for five years of labor to pay the costs.'

Although Wyatt failed to see the difference between contracted and indentured, he dropped that part of his inquiry. 'And the prisons earn a return on the criminals rather than pay for their keep at a penitentiary.'

'You got it.'

Wyatt tipped back his hat, trying to decide what he should do. 'Guess I'll get a room and wait for Mackavoy to show up. He didn't say what the job entailed, so I'm kind of stuck until he arrives.'

'Nice rooms at the hotel,' the freight office man told him.

'Thanks. I appreciate your help and information.'

The man went back to the paperwork on the counter as Wyatt went out the front door and headed for the hotel.

How about that? he thought. A combination contract and convict operation, a miniature city, with the entire population working for one single corporation! This Gaskell must be one heck of a businessman!

The young lady was a little above average in looks, clad in a faded blue dress that had seen its best days. Her dark auburn hair was pulled to the back of her head and she regarded Wanetta with a nervous look of apprehension. The wife of Locke Valeron stared back at the girl, noting she had sparkling, chromatic eyes, though presently red and tired as if from sleep deprivation.

Wanetta smiled a greeting at the girl who had knocked at her door. 'How do you do?' she said, taking note of a traveling bag sitting on the step next to the visitor. 'Can I help you, young lady?'

'I'm looking for Nessy Mason?' she replied with some hesitance. 'It is concerning the advertisement in the *Weekly Sentinel.*'

'An advertisement?' Wanetta repeated, surprised at the statement. 'In the Valeron newspaper?'

'For a nanny,' the girl informed her.

The words caused Wanetta to actually take a backward step. 'I .. I ..' she stammered uncertainly. 'Uh, let me get the child for you. She is practising her sewing in the next room.'

'Child?' The girl displayed astonishment. 'I thought she was the person requesting a nanny for *her* child!'

Wanetta bid the young lady enter and offered her a seat in the sitting room. The girl grabbed her bag and followed her inside. She placed her piece of luggage next to a cushioned chair and sat down.

'Tish!' Wanetta called down the hallway. 'Would you bring Nessy in here please?'

Wanetta's niece, Tish Valeron, entered the room with Nessy and paused to look at the new arrival – one who appeared very near her own age. She offered a smile and asked:

'Who's our visitor, Auntie?'

'This is . . .' Mrs Valeron glanced at the girl. 'I'm sorry, dear, I didn't even think to get your name?'

'Michelle Bruckner,' she informed her, 'but I go by Mikki.' Then she produced a folded printed page from the *Valeron Weekly Sentinel* and handed it to Wanetta. 'I came about the "*Help Needed*" posting in the newspaper.'

'Oh, goodie!' Nessy exclaimed. 'I didn't think I'd get one so soon!'

All three of the women gawked at her. Tish was dumbfounded, Mikki looked quite upset, and Wanetta shook her head in wonder. Tish reached out and took the paper from Wanetta. After studying it for a moment, she read it aloud.

Nanny wanted. Room and board, plus wage. Must love little girls. Inquire at the Valeron ranch for an intereview.

Tish waggled her index finger at the child. 'You didn't write this, Nessy!' she declared. 'You would never use such grown-up words.'

'Desiree helped a little,' Nessy clarified. 'I told her what I wanted and she wrote it for me.'

'Trust a new mother to want everyone in the family to have all the love she can get,' Wanetta said.

'So this is a joke of some kind?' Mikki appeared crestfallen. 'I spent every cent I had to get here!'

'No, it's no joke!' Tish told her quickly. 'Nessy is right. We often pass her around like a hot potato. A nanny is just what she needs.'

Wanetta frowned. 'Cliff is the one who should make that determination. What's he going to say about this?'

Jared Valeron, the last son living at Locke and Wanetta's home, came in the front door and stopped, having heard the last sentence. 'I caught the part about Cliff. What's he done now?' He saw the strange girl sitting in Locke's usual chair and then his eyes went to the suitcase.

'What's this? Another of Cliff's calf-eyed victims seeking compensation for her virtue and good name?'

Tish was closest to him so she was the one to punch him soundly in the arm. 'This is Miss Bruckner, Jerry. She has come about the nanny position.'

11

'The what?' he asked dumbly, rubbing the spot where Tish had hit him. 'Whose position?'

Tish giggled at her cousin's stunned expression. 'Nessy has found herself a nanny.'

Jared recovered to grunt his doubt. 'Cliff didn't say anything about hiring a child tender.'

'Exactly,' Tish told him. 'I imagine you'll want to be here when he gets the news. Being that supper is about ready, he should be along at any minute.'

'I wouldn't miss it,' Jared laughed. 'This ought to be good.'

'Listen,' the curious, deflated girl spoke up. 'If this isn't a real job, I'll. . . . .'

'You might want to wash up, dear.' Wanetta didn't allow her to question or protest. She turned to Nessy. 'As this was your idea, please escort Miss Bruckner to Wendy's old room – she can put her things in there. Then see she has water for the washing bowl and a fresh towel for her dressing table. She probably gathered a lot of dust on the trip from town and will want to clean up before we eat.'

'Sure, Grandma,' Nessy chirped cheerfully. 'I'll take special care of my new nanny.'

'Are you sure that...?' the perplexed young lady began to ask.

'Everything is going to work out splendidly, Mikki,' Tish insisted, cutting off any questions or concerns. 'I wanted to take a job in town and won't have much time to help tend Nessy. This is just what Cliff needs.'

'I agree,' Wanetta joined in. 'Though it's still a wonder that you came to us due to an ad placed by an eight-year-old.'

12

'I'm almost nine,' Nessy reminded her. 'At least, that's the day we made for my birthday.'

'I stand corrected,' Wanetta allowed. 'An ad placed by an almost nine-year-old child.'

The man was in his thirties, with a groomed mustache and neatly shorn hair. He wore a suit and a city-style hat, though he still looked out of place in this part of the country. He introduced himself to Wyatt and the two of them sat down for dinner at the Paradise Eatery.

'I can't tell you how much I appreciate this,' Clevis Mackavoy told him. 'The man I contacted in Denver said you were the one person he trusted completely.'

'And that was Police Sergeant Fielding?'

'Yes.'

'You mentioned this was only an escort duty. What am I supposed to escort?'

'Me and my two children from here to Denver.'

Wyatt frowned. 'You made the journey up here on your own. What is so different about the return trip?'

The man patiently waited as they were served their meals. Then, taking a bite first, he leaned across the table.

'I fear there may be some… difficulty in gaining the release of my kids.'

'Difficulty?'

'I previously sent a wire to Ward Gaskell. He is the owner of this company or whatever you wish to call it. I made a reasonable offer to him and it was refused. I then contacted the governor's office, but they assured me Mr Gaskell has final say on everything that takes place here in Paradise.'

'Perhaps you should start at the beginning, Mr Mackavoy. It's hard to follow a story that starts in the middle.'

Mackavoy explained that he and his two children desired passage from England to America, but he only had enough money to purchase a single ticket. He had to bring the children on board under an agreement of servitude. Indentures had been around for over two hundred years, but President Lincoln had passed the 13th Amendment to the Constitution, which put an end to slavery and indentures in America. Even so, there were a few people or companies that found a way to hire inexpensive laborers. They paid their sea fare in return for agreeing to work for several years as a contracted employee.

Having an idea of what had taken place, Wyatt asked: 'So how much money are we talking about?'

'Thirty-two dollars each for the passage here to the States. Add to that a few dollars for train fare to Colorado and delivery to Paradise.'

'And you have the money to pay their debt?'

'Many times over,' Mackavoy assured him. 'My father passed away shortly after we left England. Everything he owned was sold and the funds were sent to me. It was nearly a hundred pounds.'

Wyatt wrinkled his brow. 'And that's how much in dollars?'

'Several hundred dollars.'

'So you contacted Gaskell but he wouldn't take a fair offer?'

'The reply was from a man named Parker Sayles. He

said my children's contracts were not for sale.'

Wyatt shook his head. 'I never met anyone who was indentured, but I recall my aunt telling us something about it when she was giving the kids in our family a history lesson. Seems those people in servitude were quite often traded or sold back and forth. They were pretty much slave labor until their time was up. Then they were given a bit of money and were free to do as they pleased.

The concerned father seemed to have lost his appetite. 'You can't imagine how hard it was, Mr Valeron. It is paramount to selling your children into bondage. But there was no future for my children in London. There is little work and we would have starved. My father had a little money invested for his final years but barely kept a place for himself. I had learned a trade but could not find a job that would support my family. When my wife died, I knew I must find a new life.'

'If Gaskell turned down your offer to purchase the contracts of your kids, what makes you think he will have a change of heart now?'

'I brought more money this time, and I opened an account at Wells Fargo. I can write a pay voucher if this cost more than I have with me.'

'Thirty-two dollars each, plus a few bucks for transportation,' Wyatt recalled the contract amount. 'I would think the man would be satisfied with a hundred bucks for the pair.'

'It's why I wanted someone here I could trust. I have read stories about the west, about the outlaws and bandits, the wild savages and crooked barristers. I can't risk not getting my children safely back into my care.'

15

'A barrister?' Wyatt asked.

'Yes . . . you probably are more familiar with the terms lawyer or attorney.'

'We've got more than our share of those.'

'Anyway, I intend to open a shop for men's suits. I was an apprentice tailor back in London, but there was little to no hope of ever rising higher in the company. We were practically starving on the pittance I earned. I hope to enjoy enough prosperity so my children can finish attending school and find a good life for themselves.'

Wyatt raised a fork of food, then froze. Two men wearing badges were staring through the window of the eating house... and they were looking straight at them.

'Who did you ask about where to find me?'

'A man at the stage depot.'

'It would seem news travels fast in this burg.'

'Father!' a girl squealed. 'Father!'

Wyatt turned his head and saw an adolescent girl weaving her way between tables. She was carrying what appeared to be a drying cloth for dishes in one hand. Pixie-like, she was slender, with her hair pulled back displaying attractive features, and likely in her early teens.

'Shelly!' Mackavoy cried, rising to his feet with welcoming arms.

She dashed over to him and threw her arms around his neck.

'You came for us!' she sobbed. 'You really did!'

'I promised you I would,' Mackavoy managed the words through his constricted throat. 'I came as soon as I got enough money to pay for you and Gary's contracts.'

Shelly stepped back, practically radiant with joy, but her

16

delight dampened at once. 'I don't know, Father. No one has been allowed to leave since we arrived. The people in charge are very strict. There are a good many beatings and Gary told me he had seen a man killed – he works nights cleaning the saloon. We only see each other for a few minutes a day. I have to work here from six in the morning until closing at nine, while he works all night long every day.'

Before Mackavoy could respond to his daughter, the pair that had been watching them from the walk entered the room and marched over to their table. Both were tough-looking sorts wearing guns. Their badges had the word *Enforcer* stamped on them. The one had a cigarette hanging from his lips. He glared down at them.

'Get back to work, little scab!' he growled at Shelly. 'You ain't supposed to be talking to the customers.'

'Excuse me,' Mackavoy said politely. 'This is my daughter. I've come to pay for her release.'

The enforcer grabbed the lapels of his jacket and crammed him down in the chair he had been using. Then he pointed at the girl and snarled a second time. 'You! Get back to work!'

'Now see here, my good man. . . .'

But Wyatt put a restraining hand on Mackavoy. He forced a mellow expression to his face and confronted the two men.

'You'll have to pardon us, gentlemen,' he said without a hint of challenge in his delivery. 'We just arrived in Paradise and aren't familiar with your rules.'

Shelly hurried back across the room and disappeared into the kitchen.

'If you've business here, you both have to check in with the director of security. That's the building that houses the Paradise jail.'

'We didn't know this was different than any ordinary town,' Wyatt replied. 'I apologize for the confusion.'

'The gent here sounds right agreeable, don't he, Olmstead?' the second man spoke up for the first time. With a smirk he added, 'Maybe they just ain't very smart.'

'You could be right, Coop,' the one with the smoke sneered the words. 'Can either of you daisy-pickers read?'

Wyatt displayed a smile, although he had lowered his right hand beneath the table. Always cautious, his gun was tied down, but the riding thong was not in place. If it came to a fight, he would not be taken by surprise.

'It was our mistake, boys,' he said easily. 'I should have asked around about visiting one of your workers. As for my friend here, he only arrived a few minutes ago. We'll sure check in with your head of security and do this properly.'

Olmstead removed his half-smoked cigarette and belligerently stuck it in the middle of Mackavoy's plate of food.

Before the man could react, Wyatt again put his left hand on his employer's shoulder for restraint. He then rose slowly to his feet.

'If you're here to insist we visit the security director, you only have to say so. If, on the other hand, you're here to start a fight, we'd as soon pass. My friend here only wishes to speak to Ward Gaskell. We aren't looking for any trouble.'

'The way we do things,' Olmstead jeered, 'you don't speak to no one until the director says you can. If he sees fit, he'll let you talk to Judge Sayles. If they both clear you, then you can talk to Mr Gaskell.'

'Suits us fine.' Wyatt remained respectful. 'Do you mind if we finish eating first?'

'I think we'll take you to jail. I don't like your . . .' Coop started to draw his gun.

Wyatt's hand was a blur. He instantly covered both men before Coop could get his gun clear of its holster or finish his sentence!

'Easy, boys,' Wyatt told them in a soothing tone of voice. 'I told you, we didn't come looking for trouble . . . but no one pulls a gun on me. Let your iron slide back where it belongs.'

If Coop had been chewing tobacco, he'd have swallowed it, along with the lump of fear that went down his throat.

Meanwhile, Olmstead carefully spread out his hands. 'No need to get riled, fella,' he said, the contempt no longer in his expression or voice. 'We're just doing our jobs.'

'You said we should visit the director, so that's what we'll do,' Wyatt said, slipping his gun back to its cradle. 'My question was, can we finish our meal first or do you prefer we go there straight away?'

Olmstead took a backward step. 'Go right ahead with your meal, mister. I reckon the director can wait.'

'Obliged to you for the invite,' Wyatt said, smiling at the two men. 'Feel free to join us if you'd like.'

Both men gave their heads a negative shake. Then, like two wooden figures, they marched out of the eatery.

'By Jove!' Mackavoy exclaimed, as soon as the pair had

left the room. 'Where did your firearm come from? It appeared as if by magic!' He did not hide his amazement. 'You must be the fastest man alive at getting your weapon clear of its sheath.'

'I've done a little practice,' Wyatt told him.

'But . . . but we could have ended up in one of those disreputable gunfights, the kind I've seen on a great many book covers in the stores back east.'

'They aren't as exciting as you might think. Getting shot or killing someone should always be a last resort.'

'With your proficiency, I doubt you worry about another man's speed.'

'No amount of speed will help when someone shoots you from behind,' Wyatt informed him. 'That's why we will first try and talk things out. Are you about finished?'

'Yes, of course. I wish to get our dealing tended to and get my children out of here as soon as possible.'

'It's getting late, but let's go visit this director and see what he has to say.'

CHAPTER TWO

Cliff arrived to see Jared's horse at the hitching post in front of the house. That was unusual: Jared almost always put his horse away before supper.

Probably heading off to Valeron for some fun and games after supper, Cliff decided. It caused him to sigh. It had been weeks since he had enjoyed any recreation in town. Being a father was a full-time job, added to the full-time job he already had on the ranch. Taking in Nessy had seemed the right thing to do – and he loved her as much as if she was his real daughter – but it sure cut into a man's night life.

Rather than put away his horse, he tied the mare off next to Jared's mount. He would tend to the horse after the meal.

As he entered the house, Wanetta looked in his direction. 'Use the washroom upstairs. Nessy is using the other one.'

Cliff shrugged at her suggestion, wondering if Nessy had reached a point of modesty or something. After all, he had been helping to bathe and wash her hair since bringing her home almost two years ago.

'Hey, Cliff,' Jared greeted, passing him on the stairs.

'How's it going?'

Cliff opened his mouth to reply, but Jared went on by. Curiously, he had not only washed up for supper, he had put on a clean shirt. That was likely due to the night out he had planned, but it wasn't his cleanliness that set off an alarm in his head – it was the crooked smile on his face.

Tish happened to be putting the finishing touch on tidying up Nessy's upstairs room. She saw Cliff arrive and stuck out her hand.

'Payment please,' she said. 'Two days of watching Nessy.'

'Six-bits a day; you and Darcy are killing me,' he complained, digging out a dollar and a half.

'Maybe you ought to hire someone to look after your child,' Tish said, her face a mask of innocence. 'Be a whole lot cheaper than paying me and my sister to tend her.'

'I can believe that. It seems like I've been working for you two ever since I brought her home.'

Tish took the money and laughed. Not so much a humorous mirth, more that she, like Jared, also knew something special. She didn't offer to share the information, mincing down the stairs. She called goodbye to Wanetta and Jared as she went out the door.

By now, Cliff was growing apprehensive. He could think of no reason why Jared and Tish would be in such bang-up moods at the very same time. And what about the funny looks? It was as if they knew a joke . . . and it was about to be played on him!

Cliff washed up and went to his room, the bedroom next to Nessy's. The main Valeron home was huge, having once housed six kids. Jared had the third bedroom upstairs, but he was gone a good deal of the time. Cliff and Nessy had moved in once he formally adopted her. It was nice that she had a room to herself, and she was right next door if she had a bad dream or needed him. At present, the only vacant bedroom was Wendy's – downstairs and on the opposite side of the house from Locke and Wanetta's. Wendy had moved into town to run an accounting office and oversee several of the Valeron owned businesses.

Cliff heard Nessy's voice as he started back down the stairs. She was chattering away to someone. He might have thought it was Tish, but he had heard the door close when she left. Wanetta was in the kitchen, putting the finishing touches on the evening meal. Plus, he had looked after Jared and saw him go into the dining room. Unless Locke had returned early from his trip to Cheyenne. . . . But no, he would have seen the buggy parked next to the house.

'So who are you yakking to like an excited magpie, little princess?' he muttered aloud.

Cliff stopped near the bottom step, foot still in the air, when a young lady walked into the room – with Nessy leading her by the hand!

'Oh!' Nessy cried at seeing him. 'Daddy! Daddy! Look who's here!'

Cliff's head rotated back and forth without his conscious effort to move. 'Uh, I give up, pumpkin. *Who is* here?'

'My nanny!' she cried happily. 'Just like the one Tish read about in the storybook. Only she's way nicer.'

'Nanny?' he practically choked on the word. 'Did you say nanny?'

'Isn't she great! She knows all about the stories we've

read. She even had the very same second year reader as me when she attended school.'

'Nanny?' Cliff repeated, the title seeming to be cragfast between his eardrums and his brain.

'Cute idea having Nessy place the ad in the newspaper,' Jared taunted him. 'She did a much better job than you'd have done.'

'Nanny?' he mumbled again, still utterly confounded.

'It will be a blessing,' Wanetta joined in, entering the dining room with a kettle of stew. She smiled as she set the pot in the middle of the table. 'Mikki will move into Wendy's old room and be here for Nessy night and day.' She added: 'Except on Sundays, or when she needs a day or two off.'

'But who?' Cliff swallowed against his incredulity. 'I mean, how did. . . ?' He reached up to press a hand to his brow. 'Nessy! Did you really place an advertisement in the paper?'

'Aunt Desiree helped,' Nessy admitted. Then she clarified to Mikki. 'Though she isn't really my aunt. She is married to Uncle Brett, but he isn't really my uncle either. I just call him that. Kind of like calling Jerry my uncle, or Grandpa Locke my grandpa. They aren't really. . . .'

'That's all right, dear,' Wanetta stopped Nessy's babbling. 'We can explain all that after supper. The rolls are getting cold and so will the stew.' Then she sat down and looked to Cliff. 'As you are the last one to take your place, it falls to you to say Grace.'

'Yes, Aunt Wanetta.' Cliff remained thunderstruck, yet respectful, as he took his place next to Nessy. With everyone seated at the table, he gradually recovered from the shock of the situation. Clearing his throat, he managed a smile.

'Looks like I've got a little more to be thankful for tonight.'

Ward Gaskell was a businessman. He had a shrewd mind and could smell a nickel fifteen feet away. After the war, he had left his father's hardware business back in Missouri, a man driven to succeed. From an aide to a railroad tycoon to managing a governor's failed run for office, Ward had learned how to deal with men of all ranks. Buying a mine and striking it rich was a mere stepping-stone. He had come up with an idea of using a type of slave labor to increase profits. With more money at his disposal, it had allowed him to lend financial support to men in high positions, which, in turn, allowed him to earn even more.

He had been deciding how much the company would clear over the past month when Parker Sayles entered his office. The man looked worried, but then he always had a nervous look on his face. An ex-lawyer who left his business after he sued an innocent man into bankruptcy, Paradise had been a good place to hide from friends and relatives of the victim.

'Your enforcers got a little overeager again, Ward. I've warned you before that we need to keep them on a tighter leash.'

'Who did they beat up this time?'

He scowled his disdain. 'It's worse than that. They made fools of themselves, and a number of people witnessed it.'

'Talk,' Gaskell ordered.

Parker related what had happened when the two

enforcers pushed the wrong man at the café. He ended with, 'And now they look the dummies they are! That fast-draw artist sent them crawling away with their tails tucked between their legs.'

'Who was the guy they braced?'

'Only got a first name of Wyatt.'

'Well, it sure ain't Wyatt Earp. After all the killings at Tombstone, he went to San Francisco, chasing after some skirt. He's no longer a threat.'

'No, this guy doesn't have a big mustache either.' He sighed. 'But he was with Clevis Mackavoy, the fellow who sent us the request to purchase his children's contracts.'

'We need every single body we have, Parker. The prisons are empty and we're not getting as many new people on contracts. Not to mention, other business owners around the county have caught on to the scheme, and the shortage of people signing contracts for sea passage has caused the price to keep going up.'

'I know the situation, Ward. But the Mackavoy kids are both youngsters – thirteen and fifteen. How much good can they be? The boy won't be old or big enough to work in the mines till end of his contract. As for the girl, she will soon be the object of too many men's attention. In another year or two we'll have fights breaking out over her.'

'It's the idea of the thing,' Gaskell said. 'We let a couple kids go and others will start thinking they can contact relatives or someone else about paying off their contracts. We don't need a minuscule profit on a contract or two, we need more able workers.'

'We can hire some if need be. There are a lot of miners

looking for work.'

'Not twelve-hour shifts, six days a week, for a dollar or two a day,' he reminded Parker.

'We could cut back a little, maybe give the hired miners ten-hour days.'

'You know the problems the new men would bring with them. Miners' unions are popping up all over the country. We don't want a bunch of them coming in here and organizing our workers. How would we handle a strike? Send the prisoners back to prison and horsewhip the contracted workers?'

He snorted his contempt. 'We can't allow anyone to dictate terms to us.'

'Olmstead said he'd never seen anyone get a gun into play as quick as this guy. Do we want to buck someone like that over the custody of a couple kids?'

'Have Decker look him over and check his reputation. If he's a nobody, we can make an example out of him.'

Parker rubbed his hands together nervously. 'Seven deaths in the past two months, Ward. If the governor gets wind of the loss of life and hears of the number of beatings, he might try to shut us down.'

'The governor has too much on his plate to worry about the complaints of a few prisoners or contract workers. We need to maintain our profits. It cost a lot of money to keep enough guards and enforcers to do the job.'

'You're still doing pretty good,' Parker said. 'Another year or two and you'll have enough to retire in high style.'

Gaskell snorted. 'A man can never have too much money. By the time the ore runs out, I expect to have enough put away to never work again. I will hire a housekeeper and cook for the mansion I'll have built, a groom to tend to my horses, and a half-dozen women who will serve the rest of my needs.'

'I'm ten years older than you, Ward,' Parker said. 'I'd be happy to have enough money to hire a live-in house-keeper or even marry a dutiful wife. When you sell out and I get my ten-percent, I won't have to look very far for a willing woman.'

'It's late. Put those two new arrivals off until tomorrow. Make an excuse that I'm tied up with work, but will see them at two in the afternoon.'

'Whatever you say, Ward.'

'In the meantime, let Decker have a look-see at the quick-gun stranger. I don't intend to give up those two kids. They are both good workers and we have a valid con-tract for their service.'

'I'll pass the word to Decker and inform Mackavoy and the gunman about the appointment tomorrow. They are over with Drummer now, so he will probably find out a few other details and report to you.'

Gaskell gave a nod of approval. Then, as Parker left the office, he rotated about to the large window in the second story room. Within his view was the compound, the main street, and he could even see the constant rise of dust up the mountainside from the mine opening. He enjoyed the idea of being lord and master over his own private world. This was his empire and he controlled all of those within his personal domain. Paradise was like no other business in the country, housing over one hundred workers and running like an ordinary township.

'I have worked too hard,' he vowed aloud, 'to allow anyone to mess with my setup!'

*

Nessy was snuggled in her bed and Wanetta had turned in for the night. Jared had gone to visit his Uncle Temple – no doubt so he and Tish could compare notes and inform every Valeron who resided at any of the three main houses about the unexpected arrival of a nanny. Finally alone with Mikki, Cliff and his new employee sat down in the family room together.

'Guess we were never actually introduced,' Cliff began. 'My name is Cliff Mason. Wanetta's sister-in-law is Faye Valeron; she's married to Udal, one of the three brothers who run this ranch. Faye's maiden name was Mason; she's my mother's sister. I came to work for the family after I left home and kind of ended up adopting Nessy.' He took a moment to give her the short version of how he met the orphaned waif and took her under his care. Then he asked about her situation.

'I am also something of an orphan,' Mikki told him. 'My father died while working on the railroad. My mother never recovered from the loss and she passed away the following year. I didn't have anyone, so I was taken in by a man to look after his bed-ridden mother. The woman had a lot of money, but was dying of cancer. Her son lived with her, but he was just waiting for her to die so he could get his hands on her money. He is an evil man and was a horrible son. Once the woman died, her son found a couple who needed a child-tender for their four younger children. The eldest boy was my age, but he worked with his parents – they ran a store in town. Anyway, the other three children became my responsibility for ten-to-twelve hours

29

a day, except on Sundays. Ever since I was eleven years old, my life was tending to the house I lived in and helping raise those three children.'

'I'm surprised that didn't sour you on the idea of ever having kids or being around them,' Cliff interjected.

'Yes, well, it's something I know how to do. My schooling was quite limited, but I was educated enough so I could teach the younger boys to read, write and do their numbers.'

Cliff gave the girl a once-over peruse. Her features were actually more attractive than she presented. Hair pulled tightly back, not allowing for bangs to decorate her forehead or the hair to flatter her features, and quite pale from mostly being indoors. The fact she hadn't smiled once also detracted from her looks.

'You seem quite young to be out on your own.'

'I'm twenty.'

Cliff smiled. 'Yes, and I'm your long lost uncle.'

The girl frowned. 'I don't believe you.'

He chuckled. 'That makes us even.'

Mikki sighed and admitted, 'I turned seventeen last winter.'

'And I turned twenty-three last month,' he reciprocated. Then growing serious. 'A girl out on her own at seventeen? What does your adopted father have to say about that?'

'As I told you, the woman died the second year I was with them, and her son never bothered to adopt me,' she replied. 'In fact, he mostly wanted me to do all of the cooking and look after him besides tending kids most days. My Sundays were not a day of rest: it was a day of cleaning and laundry and sometimes entertaining him and his friends too.'

'So you ran away,' he deduced.

The girl lowered her head shamefully. 'The two older children I tended are capable of looking after the youngest of the family, and I wanted more out of life than being a personal slave to a man I despised. I put away a few cents each time I was given money to buy groceries. It took me almost a year to accumulate enough for a train ticket.'

'Won't someone be fearful you were kidnapped or something?' Cliff asked.

'I left the family and my slave-master notes and asked that they never look for me. I don't think they will.'

'Why the town of Valeron?'

'It was as far away as I could get. The town sheriff actually had to beg a ride for me from a man who was coming here to pick up some lumber. He said you had a sawmill or something like that.'

'Yes, cousin Troy oversees the processing of trees and keeping our lumberyard in town supplied. Some of the builders who need a large amount of wood make the trip out here and pick up what they need up at the mill. They get a discount for buying that way,' he explained.

Mikki moistened her lips with her tongue in an apprehensive gesture. 'Knowing my situation and my age, are you still willing to hire me?'

'Nessy seems quite taken with you.' He avoided a direct reply.

'She is a very sweet little girl.'

'I am sometimes gone for several days at a time,' Cliff informed her. 'I try to be home most nights, and the

Valerons only do the needed chores on Sundays. I'm usually home on Sunday, so you would have that day to yourself.'

'That's more than acceptable to me,' Mikki said, unable to conceal her keenness. 'I've never had an actual day off before.'

'Room and board is included, here in the main house,' he continued. 'As for payment, I have no idea how much a nanny earns.'

She shrugged. 'As I said, room and board is all I ever got.'

Cliff did some figuring in his head. 'I'm paying more to Tish and Darcy than I can afford at the moment, so what do you say to ten dollars a month?'

The girl's eyes widened and her entire face lit up. 'Oh, that would be wonderful! I was mostly hoping for a place to stay!'

Cliff realized he could have offered her less, but seeing her unbridled joy, he felt he had been more than fair. He went on with the expected duties.

'My three Valeron aunts are in charge of education. Right now, they are tutoring a handful of our hired people's children, along with cousin Martin's oldest child and cousin Lana's two kids. They are mostly younger than Nessy, but my daughter was an Indian hostage for a time. She had to relearn the English language. All of the kids here get along well together.'

'I'll see to it that she keeps up with her lessons.'

'You couldn't have brought much with you in that one little suitcase. Would you like to make a trip into town tomorrow? You could pick up whatever you need. Working

32

for us, the storekeepers will allow you credit until payday. Locke pays everyone on the first of the month, so that's when I will have the money to pay you.' He chuckled. 'I've been pretty much broke since I brought Nessy home.

'Good thing you have a house for her.'

'I'll get my own one day, but there's security for her here with Locke and Wanetta. Plus, they have the extra room, what with most of their kids being married or living on their own.'

'All but Jared?'

'Yeah, I doubt he will ever get a place of his own. Jared lives the life of a hunter and spends a lot of his time away from home. He's happiest out in the hills, sleeping on the ground, surrounded by the wilds of the mountains or forests.'

Mikki put a hand up to cover her mouth, as she could not prevent a yawn.

'Yeah, me too,' Cliff said. 'I imagine it's been a longer day for you than me. If you have any other questions, feel free to ask at any time. I'm still rather new at being a father, so anything to do with Nessy or your own situation, you only have to speak up.'

'I'd like to say how blessed I feel to be given this job, Mr Mason. I confess, it was more than a little frightening to set off on my own.'

'Call me Cliff,' he told her. 'And I know what you mean. I ended up here after I left home because I didn't want to take on the world all by myself. I've never regretted it.' He skewed his expression. 'Although the Valeron boys have sometimes used me for the butt of their jokes. They are a fun-loving bunch, but you won't find finer or more decent people anywhere.'

'I'm sure I'll like everyone on the ranch.'

Cliff grinned. 'And I can promise you, every single one of them will like you right back.'

The girl rewarded him with an actual smile as she rose to her feet. It prompted him to stand as well, and he took notice that she was much more attractive when she smiled.

'Thank you . . . . Cliff,' she murmured a bit hesitantly. 'Goodnight.'

'Yeah, goodnight to you, Mikki,' he returned. 'I hope you'll be very happy with us.'

CHAPTER THREE

The people in Paradise were not at all forthcoming about life within the secluded and controlled complex. Every question received a dubious or guarded reply. No one showed any outward hostility, but it was openly apparent the employees didn't talk about management and the contract workers or convicts kept their heads lowered and mouths shut.

'I don't like this,' Mackavoy said during their noon meal. 'How busy could Gaskell be that he couldn't speak to us? He's the boss over everyone. Besides, from the men we've encountered, he has a dozen stooges to do his beckoning. Why the delay?'

'Probably wants time to decide what he is willing to do,' Wyatt replied.

Mackavoy frowned. 'What he's *willing* to do?'

'I've dealt with powerful men before,' Wyatt told him. 'One thing stands out about them: they want control of everything and everyone.'

'Yes, but I'm willing to pay him twice what he paid to buy the indentures.'

'Consider his view of this situation,' Wyatt explained. 'He has four years left on each contract. That's eight years of free labor between them. If he is forced to replace them, how does he determine their worth? Even a youngster would cost a couple dollars a week to house, clothe and feed. Multiply that by eight years and you're talking a lot of money.'

'Good Lord, Wyatt! You don't think the man will ask for a payment like that? It would be close to a thousand dollars!'

Wyatt tipped his head to the side with uncertainty. 'Like I said, you have to look at this from his perspective. The man is bound to view this by what the loss will cost him, not what should be a fair price to recover the kid's contracts.'

'I never considered...' But Clevis halted his speech. The reason for the interruption was caused by the approach of a menacing-looking man. Wyatt revolved in his chair enough to appraise the fellow.

Average in height, the swagger denoted cockiness, along with a malevolent sneer on his face. Decked out in a immaculate black suit, expensive flat-crowned, wide-brimmed hat, highly polished boots and silver spurs, he wore two cutaway holsters for twin walnut-handled Colts. He stopped at their table, confronting Wyatt purposely.

Whenever he visited a hostile town, Wyatt was always careful to eat with his left hand, usually keeping his right hand resting on his thigh. He turned slightly further in the chair to face the newcomer squarely.

'Name's Syrus Decker,' the gent announced importantly. 'I'm Gaskell's top Enforcer.' He bore into Wyatt with a frosty gaze. 'Olmstead and Coop told me that you pulled a gun on them when they questioned you.'

'Only to prevent a misunderstanding or a fight,' Wyatt said carefully. 'We didn't come here to make any trouble; we came to buy back the contracts for this man's two kids.'

Decker regarded him with a twisted grin. 'Wyatt, ain't it? What's the rest of your name?'

'Is my name all that important? Our business is with Mr Gaskell.'

Decker did not even glance at Mackavoy. 'I asked for your whole name, honcho.' He smirked. 'It's so we can put it on your marker. I offer each man that much courtesy before I put him in the ground.'

Wyatt grinned. 'Funny, you don't strike me as being the benevolent sort who worries all that much about civility.'

'Six markers in one tidy little row,' Decker bragged. 'Each and every one with their full name . . . and the date I put them in a box.'

'Anyone of consequence?'

He frowned. 'Consequence? What's that mean?'

'I get around quite a bit,' Wyatt told him. 'If you have faced and defeated a renowned gunman, I would likely know his name.'

Decker shrugged indifferently. 'I don't much care about reputations. Them what's dead ain't likely to care if anyone's heard of them or not.'

Wyatt eased his right foot forward to straighten his right leg. It allowed the gun to be withdrawn quicker. To cover the movement, he also leaned back in the chair, also making for easier access to his weapon.

'I'm not looking for a fight, Decker,' he again told the

man. 'However, I should give you fair warning. My name is Wyatt Valeron' – he let the name sink in – 'and if you draw down on me, I'll be forced to kill you.'

Decker paused, a minute flash of recognition flickering in his eyes. He recovered his sneer immediately. 'Wyatt Valeron – the man who took the Waco Kid a year or two back.'

'You don't have to prove to me that you're a tough man with a gun,' Wyatt told him. 'We're here peacefully, looking to buy back the contract of a couple children. It's like I told you, we aren't looking for any trouble.'

Decker mulled over his options, but knew the advantage was his. He was standing upright, feet spread wide for balance. The notion of killing a man with Wyatt's reputation frittered through his brain and caused a tremor of excitement. It would mean his worth would increase; he could demand more money.

Wyatt read the conclusion and was ready. As Decker grabbed for his guns, Wyatt was also in motion.

Two shots rang out, spitting fire, lead and death!

Decker remained on his feet, but his victorious smirk had distorted into a mask of shock and surprise. He managed to glower downward at his guns... twin benign weapons that had barely cleared leather. Then his eyes rolled upwards and he pitched over onto his back, landing hard enough that the dust rose around him and settled lightly on his lifeless body.

Wyatt rose slowly to his feet and muttered regretfully to Mackavoy. 'Now we're in it.'

Locke looked up from his desk, located in one corner of the family room, as a familiar form came through the doorway to the kitchen.

'Tish?' he said, not hiding his curiosity. 'I thought you went into town to see about the job you were promised?'

'It can wait,' she said firmly, holding a note in her hand as she strode over to him smartly. 'Skip saw me ride into town and rushed over to give this to me. His runner was out delivering some mail, but he knew you'd want to see this immediately.'

Locke didn't question her further, but took the offered sheet of paper and quickly scanned the message. He uttered a groan at the news.

'Well, this is new – Wyatt needing our help! The man's been taming towns, mining camps and ending range wars for the last five years, but now he's in trouble for trying to help some immigrant.'

'Says they intend to hang him!' Tish cried, unable to hold back her fear. 'We can't let that happen!'

Locke was already rising to his feet and reaching for his hat. 'I'll ride into town and have Skip send a message to the governor. Soon as I contact him, I'll have Brett send off a wire to get some additional support.'

'What can I do?'

'Tish,' he replied to her, 'send someone to round up Jared. He is lending Troy a hand with some deliveries, so he should be at the sawmill.'

'I'll go myself!' Tish volunteered, spinning about to hurry and obey his order.

'And tell Cliff to saddle me a horse,' Locke called to her back. 'He's at the barn.'

Cliff had been supervising and helping to stain the massive building. Wyoming wind and harsh weather combined to ruin untreated lumber. As such, the Valerons kept a good coat of paint or stain on all of the wooden structures.

By the time Locke changed into his riding gear and told Wanetta where he was going, Cliff had two horses ready to ride.

'I'm going with you,' he said, not waiting for Locke to give his approval. 'I owe Wyatt more than I can ever repay. No way I'm going to sit this out.'

Locke didn't argue, but climbed aboard his favorite riding horse. Once they were pounding leather out of the yard, he cocked his head to speak to him.

'You can come along, Cliff, but I won't stand for you getting into a life and death situation. That little girl needs you.'

'I know,' Cliff agreed. 'But I can be useful in other ways.'

They kept up a hard pace for the first two miles and then slowed the horses for a breather. It gave Locke a moment to fill Cliff in on what he intended.

'What if a wire from the governor won't stop the proceedings?' Cliff wanted to know.

'Brett has some important contacts. He helped the Treasury department with a huge counterfeit operation a month or so before he met Desiree. No matter who is in office, the Treasury department will have some clout with the attorney general and support Brett's request.'

'I reckon cousin Brett will do like he did with those moonshiners a while back and pin on his old badge.'

'If necessary. We know the US Marshal's office will support his authority.' Locke shook his head. 'It might mean taking him with us, but we'll do whatever is necessary

40

to stop the hanging.'

'Wyatt surely wouldn't kill a man in cold blood, Mr Valeron. How can they figure to get away with this?'

'The cable didn't tell us much. Wyatt went with some guy to Paradise and ended up in a gunfight. I read a little about that place in the Denver paper a while back. It's not a town; it's a corporation, a massive mining operation, where they have built their own settlement. The only law is in the hands of the owner of the place.'

'Then he might not care what the governor or anyone else has to say.'

'No business wants to alienate the federal government or governor of their own state. Too many ways that sort of action can come back to cripple the company. With a request for a circuit judge to rule on the case, it should hold off any verdict until we can get people up there. Once we know what we're up against, we'll figure a way to deal with the situation.'

Cliff had no chance to ask more questions. Locke touched his horse with his heels and they reverted back to a ground-eating lope.

Parker Sayles burst through Gaskell's door without bothering to knock. Ward frowned at his entrance and gestured to the next room.

'I have a reception girl sitting outside, Parker,' he growled. 'You're supposed to let her announce you. It's hard enough for me to find things her simple mind can handle.'

The company lawyer and acting judge didn't slow his step until he reached Gaskell's desk. Then he threw down a sheet of paper.

'What's this?'

'A cease and desist order from the governor's office!' Parker cried. 'Want to know what else arrived?' He didn't wait for an answer, but slammed down a second message. 'This!'

Gaskell frowned at the writing for a moment, then his eyes bugged at the words. 'What the Sam Hill?'

'That's right!' Parker lamented. 'It's a request from the President to await the assignment of an impartial judge before we proceed with our case against Wyatt Valeron.' He threw his hands up into the air. 'The President of the United States, for crying out loud!'

'Who the hell is this guy?' Gaskell wanted to know. 'How does a gunman get the governor and the President both to take up for him?'

'I asked around before I brought you the news. Benny Janks says Wyatt and some other Valeron busted up a ranch swindle near Denver a year or so back. Then, some months ago, they also took down a crooked slaughter-house and rustling operation outside of the city. The Valeron family has more influence than we ever imagined.'

Gaskell considered their mine foreman's information. Benny was a working fool, one who had worked around Denver for a good many years. Obviously, he was a man Syrus Decker should have talked to . . . before he braced Wyatt Valeron and tried to kill him.

'Calm down, Parker,' he said, his mind mulling over solutions. 'I know how to deal with this.'

'A real judge will see what is going on!' Parker wailed.

'The beatings, the unexplained deaths, the use of contracted girls as concubines for our enforcers or at the saloon. We are gonna be closed down in about five minutes flat. We have to. . . .'

'Stop your whining like a stepped-on pup, Parker!' Gaskell demanded, his booming voice putting an immediate end to the lawyer's hysterical wailing. 'Close your mouth for two minutes and I'll tell you how we can put an end to this crisis.'

'What? How?' he wanted to know.

Gaskell quickly explained what he had in mind. Then, seeing the ex-lawyer had returned to a small degree of sanity, completed the plan by adding, 'That ought to satisfy both the governor and the President.' He snorted his contempt with an emphatic, 'Amen! The end!'

Parker's frightful mien slowly transformed to a glowing delight. Practically giddy, he almost jumped up and down. 'Yes, yes! That will do it!' He snatched up the two telegraph messages. 'I'll get those cables sent off right away!'

'And Parker?'

The man stopped before leaving and looked back. 'Yes?'

'Next time, stop and let Jane announce you. I need for her to do something besides sit and fiddle with her hair, nails or reading the latest copy of her *Harper's Bazaar* magazine.'

'Sure, Ward,' he said, smiling. 'Whatever you want.'

Gaskell watched him disappear, shook his head and uttered a sigh of relief. That had been a close call. Who would have imagined . . . the President! What kind of pull could the Valeron family have to not only sic the governor on him, but the country's most powerful man?

Jane appeared at his office doorway. 'It's boring, Ward, and a few minutes past noon. Are you taking me to lunch today?'

Gaskell looked at the clock on the wall. 'Yeah, sure, dumpling. Let me finish this last bit of work and I'll be ready.'

She flashed him a bright smile. 'OK, I'll just fluff up my hair a little and wash up.'

Gaskell watched her whirl about and mince away like a water sprite. He knew Jane was looking for more than a passing job to fulfill her contract. The liberties he had taken with her were widely known throughout Paradise. In fact, several of his top men had... companions. It kept the men happy, offered some of the more *adaptable* contracted girls far less work, and added to the overall harmony of the town. As for Jane, she had not been shy about her intentions. She had used her charm and beauty to beguile him from the moment she arrived. However, it had become more serious than he had first intended. She had even mentioned how, if she were to become pregnant, she would expect him to marry her.

He tossed aside his pencil and closed the journal. A possible disaster had been averted. He would be out a couple of good workers, but Van Stokes was bound to send a few more warm bodies in the next week or two. Until then, some of the other workers would have to fill in for the two kids.

Standing up, he smoothed his suit jacket and ran a hand over his rather sparse black hair. He kept a hat by the door, never appearing outside of his office without it. He looked younger than his thirty-six years with a hat. Those seeing his receding hairline automatically thought of him as being a few years older. With Jane being the ripe age of twenty-two, he was too old for her. Of course, wealth and power was the great equalizer. It separated a man like him from the average bend, bow, and grunt laborer. He would take the woman he wanted and only the most ignorant of fools would ever complain about his choice.

Brett Valeron handled the job of sheriff in town, so he was at the jail when his brother arrived. Jared had ridden hard and fast to reach Valeron, knowing the rescue party needed to get to Cheyenne on time to catch the train going to Denver. Seeing Brett idly sitting in the chair out front of his office, Jared suspected something had changed. He pulled up and stopped at the hitching rail.

'Where's Dad?' was the first question he directed at his brother.

'He and Cliff are over at the store, picking up a few things for Mom and the new nanny,' Brett replied. 'A few more minutes and you'd have met them on their way home.'

'What's happened?' Jared displayed confusion. 'You don't look ready to ride.'

'No need,' Brett replied. 'Wyatt is a free man.'

Jared climbed down from his horse, wrapped the reins around the hitch-rail, and followed as Brett led the way into his office. He sat down behind his desk as Jared waited for an explanation.

'It appears, Jer, either our telegraph messages or common sense changed the minds of those in power at

Paradise,' Brett began. 'A couple hours after Pa and I fired off wires to the Colorado governor and the Treasury department, I received this cable.'

He lifted up a sheet of paper and read it aloud.

'*After a thorough interview of witnesses, it has been determined that Wyatt Valeron acted in self-defense. No charges are to be filed. There will be no trial concerning the death of Syrus Decker. Pertaining to Mr Valeron's reason for being in Paradise, the matter has also been resolved. The payment for contracts of the children in question has been accepted. It is the policy of Paradise Land and Mining to ensure the fair treatment of all of its employees, whether contracted or not.*'

Brett laid the sheet of paper back down and said, 'It is signed by Ward Gaskell, sole proprietor of the PLM Corporation.'

Jared sighed his relief. 'Well, guess I made the trip for nothing.'

'Possibly,' Brett replied, seeming to withhold judgment.

Jared reached out and picked up the telegraph message, read it for himself, then held it up to his nose. 'Hum, did you take a whiff of this, Brett? Smells like day-old fish.'

Brett shrugged. 'They let Wyatt go. They let the kids out of their contracts, which is why Wyatt was there. It would seem to be a win-win for both Wyatt and his client.'

'I'm waiting for . . .' Jared said expectantly. 'What don't we like?'

Brett accommodated his cognitive state. 'I see a few unanswered questions.'

'Go ahead,' Jared urged.

'The first message was from a guy named Mackavoy. It

said Wyatt had accompanied him to reclaim his kids. Next thing, he is asking for a lawyer to defend Wyatt in a murder trial. We rush to get the support of government officials for an impartial judge and suddenly they are talking to witnesses?'

'Right.' Jared joined his logic. 'Any halfway competent lawman would check into the circumstances and talk to witnesses before any kind of charges were made.'

'Exactly.'

'And,' Jared continued, 'notice the wire states the contracts were resolved? I doubt you inquired about the issue of any contracts in your telegrams? Begs the question: what did those contracts have to do with Wyatt being charged with murder?'

'Rumors get around,' Brett told him. 'A couple weeks ago, I spoke to a man who had come to America's shores a few months back. He stopped by to get directions to our mining operation. Seems his brother hired on to work for Faro and he'd come to the States to hopefully join him. Anyway, he mentioned a joker in London who was offering to pay the passage for those who couldn't afford the fare. In return for the price of a ticket, the person had to agree to sign a contract to work for five years.'

'Indentures all over again,' Jared declared. 'That's against the law.'

'Right,' Brett agreed, 'However, an honest and legal contract is outside the scope of the Amendment. A lawyer can argue it is only a standard, yet binding, agreement between employer and a new employee.'

'Only if it's a contract a person can get out of for a fair amount of work or payment,' Jared countered.

47

'There's the crux of the matter, Jer. What if the contracts are cast in stone?'

'You seem to know more about this than me, my well-informed brother. Spill it.'

'Desiree and I took a trip to Denver a couple months before the baby came. She does enjoy music and there was a music troupe performing at the Tabor Grand Theater. While in the city, I stopped over to visit with Sergeant Fielding.' He displayed a sly grin. 'You remember him, of course, from the days of when you and Shane were hanging around at the slaughterhouse outside of the city.'

'That joke has long since worn out,' Jared complained. 'Never want to be strung up like a side of beef again . . . not ever.'

'Anyway,' Brett returned to the story, 'Sergeant Fielding said some guy arrived at the station and said he had escaped from the mines. He was seeking a lawyer who could represent him in court. It had to do with one of these contracts. According to him, the men, women and children working at Paradise were driven under the whip – literally. And if one of those contract people wanted something to eat or drink beyond what was provided by the company, the cost was so high it quickly added days to their contract. He also told Fielding how a good many people had died from beatings, and a couple had even been shot down in cold blood by the enforcers – the lawmen of sorts who keep everyone in line.'

'So what happened to the man and the case?'

'He disappeared the next day. When Sergeant Fielding sent an inquiry to Paradise, they replied the man had broken his contract and fled. They claimed to have no

48

idea where he had gone.'

'Do you believe it?'

Brett shrugged. 'If I were a betting man, I'd wager the guy's body is buried in an unmarked grave somewhere.'

'Didn't Fielding look into it?' Jared asked.

'Paradise isn't a town, it's a job site, a reputable business firm about thirty miles outside the city boundaries. It houses over a hundred people and has stores, a barber-shop, saloons, cafés, even a hotel. But it is all owned by the same big corporation. It would be like a lawman coming to investigate our treatment of the miners, sawmill employ-ees, or the cowpunchers up at the ranch.'

'Except we don't hold them prisoner because of a piece of paper.'

'It gets better,' Brett went on. 'They also employ con-victed men and women from nearby jails, asylums, or even prison. It saves the state or institution the price of housing those people and provides practically free labor for Paradise.'

'I'm beginning to think Paradise is not the right name for this place,' Jared said. 'It might ought to be called Purgatory.'

'I expect we will hear from Wyatt in a day or two. If I know him, and things are as bad as it sounds at that place, he is going to want something done.'

Jared frowned. 'This could be none of our business, Brett. I mean, we're not empowered to look into the shady dealings of a mining company.'

Brett grinned. 'Now I'm waiting for the other shoe to drop from you.'

That brought a chuckle from Jared. 'OK,' he admitted.

'I believe I'll stick around town and wait to hear what Wyatt has to say.'

'I'll tell Desiree to set an extra plate at the dinner table tonight.'

CHAPTER FOUR

Wyatt stuck with Mackavoy until he and his children boarded the train going east. As soon as it left the station, he walked down to the police station. Sergeant Fielding was at his desk and had a vacant chair waiting.

'Figured you'd darken our doorway as soon as you arrived in town,' he said, rising to offer his hand and smiling. 'Seems you Valerons always manage to get in the middle of any difficulty that comes our way.'

'We do tend to have a knack for finding trouble,' Wyatt admitted, taking his hand in a firm shake.

'Tell me what you've learned about this latest caper.'

Wyatt laughed. 'You make it sound as if our family seeks out evil deeds on purpose.'

'Well, you have been known to stick your nose into about any beehive you come upon,' Fielding said. 'I admit, this is something new. Usually you are out to tame a town or put down a feud between two factions. This? A company the size of Paradise?' He shook his head. 'My boy, that's walking barefoot through a field of cacti blindfolded.'

Wyatt agreed. 'If not for my family having some compelling contacts, I'd have wound up pricked and jabbed to death by the thorns. The trial was going to be a sham – no defense, no witnesses, only the headman's lackey pronouncing sentence. Good thing the guy running the telegraph office allowed Mackavoy to send word to you.'

'I'm told most of the people running the stores, saloon, livery and such are hired employees. We've learned about one or two who have quit in the past because they didn't care for the treatment of the workers. Even though it meant leaving a good paying job behind, those who have left were adamant they wouldn't testify against Gaskell.'

'Let me guess – they feared they might disappear if any kind of investigation got started?'

'Gaskell has a long reach and a lot of money. If it hadn't been for your pa being in good with the governor, he might not have gotten any support from his office.'

'Money does talk loud and clear to politicians,' Wyatt remarked. 'Often means the difference in winning or losing an election.'

Fielding ran a hand through his hair, showing his frustration. 'Problem is, Wyatt, we don't have a lot of influence or jurisdiction up that way. The place is a business, a mining operation. Even the US Marshals don't usually look into complaints by contracted employees or miners. It's the reason why so many miners have joined or formed unions to protect themselves from being exploited or having to work in an unsafe environment.'

'That leaves only the federal government, and we'd need proof that those contracts are a violation of the Constitution.'

'You've nailed it.' Fielding grunted. 'And that kind of investigation would take months, and you would have to have a dozen or so people lined up to testify. It's a sorry, no-win situation.'

'What about the deaths, the beatings, the mistreatment of the prisoners or the coercion of women into harlotry?'

'Harlotry?' the sergeant frowned. 'You mean prostitution?'

'One of the saloon girls admitted to me that she had been forced into service. It was that or be given to one of their enforcers. A few of the contracted girls had even produced children while fulfilling their contracts.'

Fielding's face contorted into a rigid mask. 'Anything you can prove?'

'No one dares speak up; you said so yourself.'

'I told you our hands are tied.'

Wyatt said, 'If I could provide ironclad proof of murder, beatings and forcing women into intimate servitude? Could you act?'

'With a federal warrant, we could arrest everyone involved. No legal contract gives anyone the right to commit those acts against their employees... or conscripted prisoners either.'

Wyatt got to his feet. 'Then I'll see what my family and I can do to provide you with the witnesses you need.'

Fielding groaned. 'Every time I run into one of you Valerons, I find myself standing at the edge of a precipice.'

Wyatt grinned. 'Just watch your step until we're ready. We'll keep a tight grip on your belt.'

'That's what I'm afraid of,' he joked in a morbid fashion. 'If you fall, you'll take me with you!'

*

A familiar light tap at the door told Gaskell it was his secretary.

'Yes, Jane?' he said, loud enough that she opened the door.

'Mr Sayles to see you, sir,' she announced, smiling prettily.

'Thank you, Jane,' he replied graciously. 'Send him in.'

Parker Sayles walked around Jane shaking his head. Once the door was closed, he took a chair opposite Gaskell.

'Seems a waste of effort, Ward.' Parker did not hide his annoyance. 'Why spend the time of having her announce me? I can understand anyone else, but I spend half of my working day either with you or doing your bidding.'

Rather than answer his question, Gaskell got down to business.

'Ronnie wired me from Denver this morning,' he began. 'Seems the Mackavoy family is on their way back east.'

'We expected them to leave straight away.'

'Yes, Parker, but Wyatt Valeron went to visit the Denver police.'

The man shrugged. 'So what? It was probably just to make sure there would be no problems due to his being charged with murder.'

'We can't be sure of that. I don't trust that Valeron character.'

'You mean because he helped save that woman and her ranch? The one who had been stuck in a lunatic asylum?'

54

'Don't forget the rustling ring and slaughterhouse a few months back.'

Parker's expression began to darken. 'You don't think Wyatt Valeron would try and take us on? I mean we don't fall under any local law's jurisdiction. We're using duly assigned prisoners and legally binding contracts for everyone but the hired employees. We're not breaking any laws.'

Gaskell harrumphed. 'No laws! How about the graveyard west of town? How about a dozen cables or letters asking about missing loved ones the past year? How about the fact we've induced some of the women to serve in the saloon or submit to the whims of our enforcers?'

Parker was taken back at his passionate tone of voice and the reddening of his face. He suddenly realized Gaskell was scared. He didn't like that, not one bit. If he was frightened, there was dire concern for his own neck and the others as well.

'Do you know what Valeron had to say? I mean, when he went to talk to the law?'

'No, but his next stop was the telegraph office. Ronnie claims it would mean a prison sentence to try and bribe anyone in that office for information. The owner is an honorable sort who would likely report him to the law.'

'It sounds as if Valeron is staying in town.'

'At the Grand Hotel. Ronnie did learn from one of the maids that Wyatt had rented a room without giving a date for when he was leaving.'

'Could it be to check around for another job?'

Gaskell noted the hopeful look on Parker's face. However, he didn't trust luck or chance. 'I told Ronnie to keep an eye on him. If he takes another job, OK. But if it looks like he's going to make trouble for us, we will have to deal with him.'

Parker's eyes broadened with alarm. 'We're talking about a Valeron, Ward. You don't up and kill a man whose family has the ear of both the governor and the President of the United States!'

'If it comes to it, I will make sure nothing leads back to us. Wyatt has tamed a few towns and made a number of enemies. I'm sure we can figure a way to put the blame elsewhere.'

'For the sake of the company and both of our lives, I hope you know what you're doing.'

'Rest easy, my friend,' Gaskell said, attempting to sooth his worries. 'I didn't get where I am today by risking my neck every time a problem arose. For the time being, we will sit back and watch the man. So long as he doesn't try anything against us, we've no reason to retaliate against him.'

'When do you expect another shipment of bodies for the jobs we need filled?'

Glad to move on from the Valeron topic, Gaskell looked at a calendar of the month, courtesy of Jane's limited handiwork, which he had pinned to the wall. Although it looked like a child's paper from primary school, it did have the right number of days for the month.

'The next ship is due in about a week,' he surmised. 'Should be at least a dozen or so new people coming.'

'With ships arriving almost daily from other countries, it's a shame we only have one man signing people up.'

'Van Stokes has to be careful,' he reminded Parker. 'One wrong word to a ship captain who won't take a few dollars to turn a blind eye . . . that's all it would take to shut us down.'

'The law doesn't prevent people from signing and ful-filling a contract,' he argued. 'We are well within our rights.'

'So long as no jackleg lawyer sticks his nose into the details. Even indentures could be bought, traded or sold, and anyone could buy one for the right price. I don't think our contracts would stand up in a real court of law . . . say, before Congress or a state-appointed attorney.'

Parker threw up his hands in exasperation. 'But we let the kids go, Ward! It's proof that we are within the guide-lines of contracted employees!'

'Yes, under pressure from both the state and federal government. Not exactly a voluntary endorsement of the law.'

'Then we do what – sit on our hands and wait?'

'Ronnie will keep an eye on things in Denver. If the wind starts to blow our direction, we will know ahead of time.'

'OK. Fine.' Parker harrumphed. 'Business as usual, except we are another two bodies short.'

'If need be, hire the next people who come through looking for work,' Gaskell said. 'Once we get a few new contract employees from Van Stokes, we can always let one or two of them go.'

Parker rubbed his chin. 'I don't know, Ward. All of the people working for us know the situation and are willing to keep their mouths shut. New hires might not see the treatment by some of the job foremen or enforcers as humane.'

Gaskell was growing tired of the conversation. With some irritation he barked, 'Just do it!'

The sharp tone of voice was enough to cow Parker. Again, he raised his hand, this time in a gesture of surrender. 'Sure, Ward. Whatever you say. I'll tell Drummer to keep an eye out for any job hunters who come through.'

'Contact the prisons and jails again,' Gaskell suggested. 'We have several inmates whose time is about up. We don't dare keep any of them beyond their release date.'

'I'll do it, but some of the judges are getting soft. They give these people such short sentences it's hardly worth the price of transporting them here.'

'I agree,' Gaskell said. 'Anyone serving less than sixty days, let's not bother with. By the time they are trained to do a decent job, it's time to turn them loose.'

'I haven't kept track – how many miners are due to leave this month?' Parker wanted to know.

'Three prisoners and one of our first contract workers.'

He flinched from the news. 'We better hope a lot more people can't pay their debts or get caught for non-violent crimes. Otherwise, we'll have to hire more miners.'

'We can hope Van Stokes has several replacements coming, but don't count on it. Like I said, hire a few workers that are needed and pay the going rate.'

'I'll speak to Drummer; he can spread the word.'

'How about a replacement for Decker?'

'We've a couple guards who might do the trick. None of them are as good with a gun as Decker, but he was a little overzealous.'

'Too damned overzealous,' Gaskell agreed. 'He killed that one Spaniard for calling him a murderer.' The town owner snorted. 'Tough way to win your point, being shot down in cold blood.'

'I'll have Drummer pick a couple of men to talk to. He knows which ones he can control.'

'You and Drummer both handle the interview. I don't want another wild man like Decker.'

'My thinking as well, Ward. We'll make sure the replacement understands the job.'

Gaskell waved his hand to dismiss Parker. The man left the room and Gaskell walked to the window that overlooked his city, his compound, his corporation. The misfortune of having Wyatt Valeron show up should be but a single bump in his road to wealth and position. He would hope the man was satisfied with having helped Mackavoy get back his children. However, the Valerons had a reputation for sticking their noses into other people's business, especially when there was something awry with that business. He would stay watchful and keep on his toes until he was certain the wandering do-gooder was out of his life.

Jared and Brett discussed the message from Wyatt as they sat down to eat supper.

'What about involving the Pinkertons?' Desiree spoke after setting a plate of roast pork on the table. 'They could slip a man inside the Paradise company and get the evidence you need.'

'You know they don't usually get involved with much other than railroad trouble this far from their headquarters,'

Brett replied. 'I'm sure you recall the combination praise and cussing out you received when you helped us at Brimstone.'

She laughed at the memory. 'Couldn't very well reprimand me. I quit to marry you.'

'The baby still asleep?' Jared wanted to know. 'I haven't held the little nipper since he was born.'

'He's still a baby,' Desiree said meaningfully. 'He isn't ready to go hunting with you or learn to shoot a gun just yet.'

Jared grinned. 'There are other things I can teach him – gambling, teasing girls, or knowing when to wet on his daddy's lap.'

'He already knows that trick,' Brett quipped.

'But he can certainly do the same for you,' Desiree joked. 'I'll let you hold him after he's drank a bottle of water. It goes through him like a hollow tube.'

'Speaking of tricks,' Jared said, grabbing hold of Brett's use of the word. 'Whose idea was it to put an ad for a nanny in the local paper?'

Desiree displayed a playful mien. 'Did the girl show up? Did Cliff hire her?'

'Yes to both questions, though you missed seeing the most perplexed expression ever to cross cousin Cliff's face.' He laughed. 'For all of his charm and beguiling ways with women or girls, Cliff was completely dumbstruck when he met the new nanny.'

'Got to hand it to Nessy,' Brett said. 'Tish left her to visit with us while she went to talk to Skip about working at his store. The little tyke complained to Desiree how she was really going to miss her. Seems that Tish has been doing most of her tending around the ranch.'

'So she asked if I could sometimes visit,' Desiree joined in on the story. 'I told her that I had to care for the baby, and she said something about wishing she had a big sister to look after her all the time.'

'Next thing,' Brett chimed back in, 'the two of them are writing an ad for the paper.' He grunted his surprise. 'Wasn't an hour after the paper was printed that Miss Bruckner was knocking at our door and asking directions to the ranch. I knew Charlie Gates was going to the sawmill, so I got her a ride.'

'She looked pretty young to be out on her own,' Jared pointed out. 'Bet she isn't much over sixteen.'

'We didn't have a lot of time to talk to her,' Desiree said. 'Brett had to catch Charlie before he got out of town.'

'Well, she's a fixture now. The girl and Nessy really hit it off. By the time Cliff got home from work, the decision had been made. He pretty much had nothing to say about it.'

Desiree said, 'I hope she works out. She seemed a nice girl.'

They had continued to eat while they talked. When Brett finished his meal he pushed back from the table.

'What do you think, Jerry?' he wanted to know. 'It sure looks like Wyatt is going to try and help those people at Paradise.'

'I've an idea that might help the cause,' Jared replied. 'You might need to call in a favor or two from the US Marshal's office. And it will take a few volunteers . . . Faro as well.'

'Faro?' Desiree inquired. 'But isn't your cousin about as

bungling with a gun as I would be trying to rope a wild mustang?'

'Won't need him for his fighting prowess,' Jared said. 'Wyatt will sure enough keep an eye on his younger brother.'

'You've piqued my interest,' Brett admitted. 'Tell me what you have in mind.'

Locke had asked Faro to join Jared, Cliff, and the family for dinner. Faro spent most of his time up at the coalmine, although they did have a smaller mine that produced enough ore to turn a profit. Between the two places, he hardly ever had time for family get-togethers. He knew something of importance was brewing, as Locke didn't often include him in family problems.

Once the meal was out of the way, Locke led the other three men into the family room. Nessy went to play in her room until Mikki joined her. Mikki had stayed to help Wanetta clear the table and do the dishes.

'OK, Uncle Locke,' Faro spoke, unable to wait any longer. 'What's going on? Why the invite?'

Jared was the one to reply. 'We need your expertise, cuz,' he said bluntly. 'How'd you like to become a mine inspector for a few days?'

That put a shocked look on his face. 'Me?' He laughed at the notion. 'Geez, Jer, I don't know beans about being an inspector. Our two mines are the only ones I've ever been around.'

'Yes, but I remember Uncle Udall telling me you did a lot of reading on the subject. And the one time I went with you to the ore mine, you told me all about sulphides, heavy metals, pyrite and all that stuff. Plus, you can spout the right terms about support beams and the use of narrow gauge rail cars.'

Faro shrugged. 'Yeah, I know a little, but not enough to fool an actual mine inspector. They know how to look for stress points and can name most every kind of different rock at every level of a shaft.'

'You can spout technical jargon,' Jared countered.

'It isn't that easy,' Faro argued. 'Some hard-rock mines need almost no supports and other have to be propped up every foot of the way. Then there's the chutes, and chimneys, the ladder-ways or shafts, cross-cuts or winzes – a dozen more things like that, stuff I've never had to deal with. Our mines are about as simple as you will find anywhere.'

'But they are safe,' Locke interjected. 'Not one major cave-in or loss of life since we started mining. Not many companies can claim the safety rate you've managed.'

'Yes, but that's because we're not trying to get rich. We don't cut corners. We don't blast without taking every safety precaution. No big mining operation would spend the extra amount of time and resources we do. They want to earn the maximum dollar on ever ounce of ore.'

'Come on, Faro,' Jared jibed. 'You've always been something of a prig. When the aunts and Mom were teaching us our history, English and math, you made a point of always getting the best scores.'

'Not in math,' Faro argued. 'Martin had the brain for that.'

'All right, maybe not in math, but he never lorded it over us like you did.' Faro put on a look of affront, but

Jared prevented his rebuke by raising a hand. 'And I'm not complaining one bit. In fact, that's what we need – someone who can pass as being college educated, the kind of guy who thinks he knows it all. It's exactly what we want.'

'Holy cats, Jer!' Faro snorted. 'You really know how to sugarcoat an offer! I've got to throw in with Wyatt. He once told me that no woman would ever be able to live with you because you're too dad-blamed blunt!'

'This is for a good cause,' Locke spoke up. 'Jared might have the tact of a charging buffalo, but he has the right goal in mind.'

Faro's face worked as he thought over the notion, then he glanced at Cliff. 'What's your part in this, Clifford? Do they have a girl they want you to seduce?'

He rewarded the question with a wry grin. 'Nothing so glamorous, Faro. I get to hold down the ranch, along with my adopted daughter and our new nanny!'

Wyatt and Martin's younger brother finally cracked a grin. 'I do believe Uncle Locke is offering me the easier chore.'

Cliff grunted. 'Of that, cuz, I haven't the slightest doubt!'

CHAPTER FIVE

Brett Valeron, Sergeant Fielding and a government inves-
tigator named Bryles were among those waiting at the
dock when the transport ship arrived from England. As
soon as the gangplank was in place, the three men
boarded.

There were a sizable number of people gathered about,
awaiting the crew to allow them to disembark. However,
Fielding spoke to the man in charge and told him there
would be a ten-minute delay. The ruse was that they had to
check for any disease on board and needed time to inspect
the passengers.

The captain, a man named Preston, arrived in a huff.
Rather small in stature, the man made up for it with
bluster.

'Who the hell do you think you are?' he bellowed.
'We've no plague or pox aboard. I know the rules. I would
have informed the authorities upon our arrival if. . . .'

'Ease up on the helm, Captain,' Bryles said, raising his
hands to stop his protest. 'Let's have a word in private and
then we will shortly be out of your hair.'

Once the three of them were in his cabin, Brett produced a contract from Paradise, the one the missing laborer had given to Sergeant Fielding before disappearing. The captain recognized the paper at once and his ostentation disappeared.

'How much do you earn for each of these contracted people that come aboard your ship?' Bryles asked frankly. 'We know you are allowing people to travel on credit, as long as they sign one of these.'

'I . . . I. . . .' He cleared his throat. 'They arrive with a man in London. He vouches for the people and gives me their signed contracts. Upon arrival here, a representative from Paradise pays for their passage.'

'How much do you earn on these contracts?' Bryles remained stern. 'Give me an exact amount.'

'The fee charged is thirty-eight dollars each.'

'So you make six dollars a head for each of these indentured servants?' Brett said.

'Only three,' he muttered in self-defense. 'The man on the other end gets the same. If the owner of this ship knew I was allowing people to ride without first having the fare in hand, I could end up fishing off of the pier instead of captaining a ship.'

'Speaking of the man on the other end, when does he get his payment?'

The captain sighed in defeat. 'I'm given a pouch when the group is picked up. I take my share, cover the cost of the fares, and return the balance to London. The man at that end gets his money upon my arrival and lines up passage for other contract employees at that time.'

'He'll get nothing but a severe warning this time!' Bryles

announced. 'If you want to avoid a charge of promoting slavery, you will cooperate with us one hundred percent!'

'Slavery?!' he cried. 'I only transport people on credit. I've no part in the handling of these contracts!'

'The law against indentures is very clear,' Bryles fired back. 'You could end up in jail over this.'

The man paled at the notion. 'Now, wait a minute,' he said meekly. 'I'm cooperating. Whatever you need, I'll be glad to . . .'

Bryles announced: 'We are relieving you of these passengers and there will be no payment made to you or the mangy scoundrel working over in London.'

'But . . . how do I cover the fares of a dozen people?'

'Out of your own pocket, Captain,' Brett spoke up. 'We will see to the contracted subjects and you will cease providing passage for any more contracted laborers.'

Preston glowered at him. 'This is going to cost me a fortune!'

'If you wish to contest our actions, we can settle this in front of a judge,' Brett replied. 'But be forewarned: it will end with you losing this ship and spending a few years behind bars.'

Totally intimidated now, the captain bobbed his head. 'Whatever you need. I didn't think there was anything wrong with contracted labor. It's been going on for years.'

'Not this kind of contract – this agreement allows no rights or privileges for the individuals. This is nothing more than a form of slavery.'

Captain Preston gulped at the word slavery. No way was he going to end up before a magistrate and face that charge!

'What's the name of your contact here – the man with your money?'

'Name's Van Stokes, and he usually has a couple of men with him. They take charge of the contracted people and escort them to the train. Once they have purchased tickets for the passengers, the two men accompany them westward. I don't know where Van Stokes lives. He is always waiting on the dock.'

Brett looked at Bryles. 'We need a complete list of your contracted people. Then we are going to meet with Van Stokes.'

The government man agreed. 'Get to writing, Captain. One slip on your part and your next bunk won't be in the captain's quarters, it'll be in a prison cell!'

Faro Valeron had never been much for the adventuresome and often rowdy games his cousins played. Wyatt would join in, but he and his brother, Martin, usually played by themselves or kept company with Nash. All three of them were more prone to using their heads rather than brawn. Martin had taken up accounting and a bit of law, while Nash had become a doctor. For Faro, he loved to dig and explore old ruins or caves. He often spent his spare time reading stories about archaeologists and the search and discovery of lost cities around the world. Thankfully, his father, Udal, recognized his and Martin's ambitions. When the family found coal in the nearby hills, they put Faro in charge of the mining operations. Shortly thereafter, other ore deposits were discovered on their land. He hired a geologist to test the area and soon had both operations going. There was no huge bonanza of rich ore, but they mined enough to pay for their efforts and show a profit. As for coal, that was a necessity, being that it took too much timber to fill the needs of fuel for their ranch and the nearby town.

Conferring with Jared, Wyatt, and Sergeant Fielding, Faro felt completely out of place. It was like sitting in on one of the rowdy games of their youth. Jared had been involved in all manner of chaotic and deadly adventures, and Wyatt had settled several feuds and tamed more than one wild town. However, both of his cousins recognized Faro was a different breed of man. There was no more than the usual teasing and joking between them than if it had been Shane or Reese joining them.

'Anyone see you?' Fielding asked Wyatt, once Faro had been introduced.

'I've still got a shadow. I believe there are two or three of them, but I lost the one watching me an hour or so ago. Got him to thinking I was going to take a ride, then slipped away when he went to round up his horse.'

'Gaskell's men?' Fielding ventured a guess.

'Gotta be,' Jared was the one who answered. 'I got a look at one of them and he could have been sired by a weasel.'

The four of them had met up at the police headquarters and were in a room to themselves, out of earshot or sight of any passers by. Fielding was in charge and invited a fifth man to join them. The fellow appeared to be in his mid-twenties, average in looks and size, but owned a serious brow and speculative brown eyes. He was lithesome, yet appeared coordinated and athletic.

'You Valerons,' Fielding said, presenting the young

man, 'this is Officer Munson. He is going to pose as Faro's assistant. I chose him because he is new to our police force, having just moved here from St Louis. This being his first week with us, I very much doubt the spies for Gaskell have seen him.'

'How-do,' Munson greeted them. 'I've heard a few stories about you boys from the Sarge here.'

'What brings you this far west?' Jared wanted to know. 'Not enough action in St Louis?'

'I had a conflict with a superior.' He shrugged. 'Put a wife-beater in the hospital during an arrest and he caught the blame from the mayor's office. I knew that, so long as I was working under him, I'd never get a promotion to detective. My uncle settled in Golden, so I checked around to see if they or Denver needed an experienced officer.'

'Know anything about mining?' Faro asked. 'I'm a little shy on experience in any mines other than our own.'

'Sorry,' Munson said. 'You'll have to tell anyone who asks that I'm new at the job.' He gave a helpless gesture, then added: 'But I do write pretty good and my spelling is better than average.'

'Your purpose is diversionary,' Fielding reminded him. 'Brett and Jared will be the ones sticking their necks out. You will only need to find enough things wrong with the mine to keep Gaskell's attention.'

'When is Brett due back?' Faro asked no one in particular.

'He should be arriving by train tomorrow or the next day,' Jared replied.

'Then I'm to leave before you and him?'

'You head out first thing in the morning, cuz,' Jared advised him. 'Brett will likely need a day to rest up from the long train ride.' He laughed. 'Sure glad I didn't have to make that trip with him. I'm not a big fan of trains.'

'Any questions about your job?' Fielding questioned Faro.

'I do know much of the necessary lingo,' Faro offered, 'and a prison gang will likely have a few ex-miners. I can probably direct my questions so as to get a little information from them concerning mine safety.'

'When their new arrivals don't show up, it might put them on guard,' Wyatt posited. 'They have several of their enforcers watching the town day and night. You'll have to be ready to talk quick and make them believe you have the power to do what you say.'

'You've got all you need,' Jared said. 'The letter from the governor's office states that you are a mine inspector. It gives you the authority to poke around and make a nuisance of yourself.'

After discussing the assignment for another hour, the group broke up. Faro and Munson left together. The two of them would get rooms at the hotel to cover the story that they were working in tandem.

Wyatt turned his room over to Jared and made sure his shadow saw him exit the hotel with his travel bag. With him leaving town, it was hoped it would lower the awareness of Gaskell's watchdogs. Wyatt would head home for a visit with his family and stay available until called upon.

Cliff found himself hurrying to get home early each night. It warmed his heart that Nessy immediately took to Mikki.

The two of them seemed more like sisters than a nanny and her charge. He often watched when neither of them knew he was around, filled with gratification that here was a young woman who served not only as a caregiver and friend, but took on the role of teacher and mother.

Cliff discovered something else, an awakening deep inside, a surreal yearning he'd never known before. Ever since he entered his teen years, he'd flirted with and lusted after girls and women, instilled with the desire to relish their favors. Reflecting on his past, he'd had numerous encounters or conquests. But there had been no real love, no intent to make a lifelong commitment with any of them. The feelings that surfaced when he looked at Mikki were different. He didn't see her as a short-term prospect, a taste of wine to sip and discard. This girl evoked in him a desire to not only have and to hold . . . but to keep.

There came an opportunity to explore a more intimate relationship one night after Nessy had gone to bed. Locke and Wanetta were next door, playing cards with Temple and Gwen, Tish and Shane's parents. With Jared away from the ranch, only the nanny, Nessy, and he remained in the house.

Mikki had gotten into the habit of drinking a cup of tea before she went to bed. Cliff didn't care much for the drink himself, but he knew how it was made. He had it waiting when the girl came into the kitchen.

'Ready for your nightly libation?' he asked, pouring the tea into a small cup.

'Yes, thank you,' Mikki said, displaying appreciation for his consideration. She took a chair at the small kitchen table.

Cliff set a small container with cream next to the sugar bowl, so they were both within her reach, then took the chair opposite her.

'You've had a few days to get used to the Valeron ranch and home,' he opened the conversation. 'Do you think you're going to be happy with us here?'

'Oh, yes,' she said, her eyes shining brightly. 'This is like a special haven or sanctuary, away from the rest of the world. You are fortunate to be a part of such a wonderful family. I've yet to meet anyone I didn't like.'

'My side of the family was not so large. I only had one brother growing up, and he was bigger and older than me. Rodney married a newspaper woman and has made a good life for himself.'

'What about you?' Mikki asked. 'Darcy told me you have had a great many girlfriends, but never one that turned serious.'

Cliff felt his outlook plummet. 'You've been talking to Darcy?'

'She is often around tending her mother's garden or visiting here with Mrs Valeron. She also watches over some of the children when Nessy is playing with them.'

She's got a big mouth too! Cliff groaned inwardly.

Mikki paused and made eye contact. Confirming his fears, she ventured what Darcy had told her. 'She warned me that you were quite . . .' she searched for the term she wanted, then finished with, '*comfortable* around less-experienced girls.'

Cliff raised his hands in a sign of surrender. 'I don't deny it,' he said. 'I have spent much of my adult life chasing after girls. But,' he hurried to clarify, 'that all changed when I adopted Nessy.'

Mikki's facial expression revealed her doubt.

'I mean it,' he reiterated. 'I was a prime woman-chasing fool up until Nessy came into my life. I confess that I courted and played upon the affection of a number of girls. I didn't respect womanhood nor motherhood – not until I became a father.' Heaving a sigh, he shook his head. 'But, like I said, Nessy changed my life, my outlook on life, and my opinion of women. I've not even looked at a pretty girl since meeting Nessy.' He grunted with a mock humor. 'I haven't had time, not for much of anything since I adopted her.'

'So I shouldn't take Darcy's warning to heart?'

He laughed. 'Actually, she had every right to warn you – I admit to a terrible past history with women. However, next time you speak to her, you might ask her if she knows of any girls I've been chasing after recently. She won't be able to point a finger at any of them, because I've stopped looking for a quick romp with a willing girl. I'm no longer interested in a simple conquest or a girl to spark just for the fun of it.'

'So now you are interested in a serious, long-term relationship?'

'First of all, when I look at you, I see a young woman, but not necessarily an experienced girl.'

He noticed how she lowered her eyes – a sign of admission or embarrassment. 'I say that only because I don't wish for you to see me as the man I used to be. And in answer to your question, I've become more interested in what kind of woman would be a good wife and mother – one who would accept Nessy as her own child. I realize that's a lot to ask of any woman.'

'Darcy mentioned there were several on this ranch who would jump at the chance to marry one of your family.'

Cliff shrugged. 'I've kidded and flirted with two or three of those girls, but it was mostly in fun. Like I said, I've never really been serious about a woman.'

'Why are you telling me this?'

'Mikki,' he said, instilling all of the honesty he could muster, 'it's because I don't think of you in the same way I used to think of those girls.' He again raised his hands, as if to stop her from replying or rebuking his words. 'Don't get the wrong idea. I'm not asking to court you. That would be totally unethical, what with you being a nanny to my daughter. Any, uh ... romantic inclinations would have to be mutual and handled delicately. You don't know me all that well yet, and I really don't know much about you.'

'Why mention it at all, if you're not . . .' again, she hesitated to select the right word, 'interested in courting?'

'Because I am interested in you,' he admitted. 'That's the problem. I don't want you thinking I'm the same guy I used to be. It isn't about how I've changed; it's more that I've grown up. Being a father has made me see how important a woman is, that it's more than a flirtation or bit of fun. I want − I need,' he corrected, 'a woman who will be both a wife and mother. I've never looked for that in a girl before.'

Of all the reactions Cliff might have expected, tears filling the girl's eyes was not on the list. She lowered her head and swallowed, as if she had been chewing and tried to swallow a much too big of bite to get down.

'I. . . .' Her voice cracked and she swallowed a second time. 'You don't know the truth about me,' she barely murmured the words.

'Truth? What are you talking about?'

But the girl rose up abruptly. 'I . . . I can't!' was all she said. Then she ran from the room and down the hall to her bedroom.

Cliff stared after her and went over the last few words between them. What in the world had he said wrong? He had always been the guy who had women all figured out. His wit and charm made winning a gal's affection almost too easy. But Mikki? She was a conundrum, a riddle with no clues. That was something he had never faced before.

Drummer, as head of security for Paradise, led Faro and Munson into the main building at the center of town. The three men entered an office with a shingle reading: 'Parker Sayles, Judicial Magistrate'. A man was seated at a desk, smoking an oversized cigar – made more conspicuous due to him being smaller than most men. He sported slicked-back hair and a narrow mustache, attired in a tattered, but once expensive, gray suit. He regarded Drummer with a scowl, obviously unhappy he had simply walked in without stopping to knock on the closed door.

'What is it, Mr Bonheur?' he asked, oozing with his own importance. 'Who are these men?'

'They's from the state,' Drummer replied. 'They's got a letter to show you.'

Parker's pale-green eyes swept over the pair. 'What kind of letter are we talking about?'

Faro stepped forward and stretched his hand out with

the document. Parker impudently snatched it from his fingers and scanned the writing.

'The governor's office?' His frown was offset by his puzzlement. 'A state inspector?'

'Mine safety,' Faro announced. 'The state has mandated all working mines be inspected for safety. It's an attempt to cut down on the number of injuries caused by unsafe working conditions.' Faro took on a more severe look. 'The deaths reported from your mining operation far exceeds the norm, Mr Sayles. It is the governor's intention that we correct whatever problems we can.'

'And what gives you such insight to inspect our diggings?'

'I've been working at or operating both ore and coal mines since I turned sixteen,' Faro told him truthfully. 'Once I became foreman, we suffered only minor injuries and haven't had a death in the past three years. My safety record is the reason the governor chose me for this job.'

'And this other man?'

'In training to also become an inspector. There are far too many mines for me to cover on my own. Once he has seen enough digging sites he will inspect mines on his own.'

Parker shook his head. 'I'm not sure about the legality of . . .'

'This falls under state jurisdiction, Mr Sayles,' Faro cut him off sharply. 'You have no say one way or the other. Either cooperate or I'll shut down your mining operation.'

'Uh. . . .' His arrogance waned. 'I'll have to speak to Mr Gaskell. He's the owner of . . .'

'Speak to whomever you wish,' Faro was again curt. 'My

assistant and I are going to rent a room at your hotel. Then we will have something to eat. Once we have finished the meal, we will begin our inspection. I suggest you inform the men in charge to be ready to accommodate our inspection. As I said, you have no say in the matter – it is the law!'

Without another word, Faro and Munson left the office. Once out to the walkway in front of the building, they started off towards the hotel.

'I gotta say,' Munson muttered under his breath. 'You got more brass than the biggest band in Colorado.'

'It's something I learned from my brother Wyatt,' Faro replied quietly. 'Walk the walk, talk the talk, and never look back.'

'And that works all the time?'

'Except when he's ended up having to kill or be killed to back up his stance,' Faro joked morbidly. 'That's the single downside to Wyatt's philosophy.'

Munson coughed his dismay. 'That's a very big downside, Faro.'

'You wanted a little more excitement,' Faro reminded him. 'Here's your chance.'

Gaskell was fuming, stomping about the room and cursing at the top of his lungs. 'A state inspector?' he howled. 'Since when does the government care about a few miners?'

'It's probably due to using prisoners in our workforce,' Parker said. 'The five or six who have died were all listed as accidental deaths in the mines.'

'Yes, I know,' Gaskell snapped. 'Can't very well tell the

truth that a couple were killed trying to escape, another man or two from the exhaustion of the hard work, and Decker and his men killed another two or three for getting out of line.'

'We're having one crisis after another, Ward. This is getting serious.'

'Better have someone warn Janks.'

'I told Drummer to talk to him about the inspection. Benny Janks knows about mining and safety. I'm sure he can deal with the inspector.'

'How much do we trust him?' Gaskell asked. 'Janks has done some complaining in the past.'

Parker shrugged. 'He knows the consequences of getting out of line. We pay him a good wage to run the mining crew.'

'Tell him there will be a bonus for him if this goes away quietly,' Gaskell said.

'I'll see to it, Ward.' Then he frowned. 'You think this might have something to do with Adams?'

Gaskell recalled the miner who had run off and tried to get help in Denver. Luckily, Ronnie had taken care of that little problem before charges could be made against anyone in Paradise.

'He did stir things up, but it's been several months. I think it's more likely that Valeron reported what he'd seen while he was here.'

Parker wasn't convinced. 'The man spent more time in jail than he did snooping around. If not for the drink at the saloon, while waiting for Mackavoy to collect his kids and their belongings, he didn't talk to hardly anyone.'

'Yes, but Mackavoy's two kids knew a lot about what was

going on. They even witnessed a beating or two.'

'What can they do?' the judge asked. 'Those kids are too young to testify in court, and Adams disappeared before he could do much more than throw around a few accusations. The law probably thinks he made up the story as a way to get out of fulfilling his contract.'

Gaskell thought over Parker's theory. It fit the circumstances, and no one of authority had come nosing around about Adams. Of course, that was before a Valeron got involved in their operation.

'Those blasted Valerons! A bunch of interfering, philanthropic snoops seeking sainthood! I wish we'd have strung up Wyatt Valeron before any of his family's powerful friends had a chance to react.'

'Too late for that now, Ward. Besides which, this might have nothing to do with them.'

'I suppose you're right. Nothing we can do at the moment but wait and see. Tell the others to keep their eyes open. Also make a point of telling Drummer that he and his men need to check every stranger who turns up. Find out what they want and why they're here. Until this blows over, we don't want any surprises.'

CHAPTER SIX

Reese listened to Cliff's story about Mikki's odd reaction during the moving of a small herd of cattle.

'I don't care for the idea of you trying to woo Nessy's new nanny,' Reese said. 'There is such a thing as proper behavior between a man and his hired help.'

Cliff shook his head. 'No, it ain't like before, Reese. I wasn't trying to . . . to court her exactly. Besides, I . . . well, she's different from all of the other girls I've met. I see her as something special.'

'She's still your employee and seems pretty young.'

'Reese,' Cliff sighed, 'I've always been a total scoundrel when it comes to women – ever since I kissed my first girl. But this time it feels completely different. I don't want a one-night good time with this girl. Mikki strikes me as too good for that sort of thing.'

Reese frowned in thought. 'Come to think on it, you haven't done much skirt chasing since Nessy entered your life.'

'Entered?' He laughed. 'Dad-gum, she plum took it over! She's been my all-consuming concern since the court granted me custody of her.' He clicked his tongue. 'And that wouldn't have happened without Locke and Wanetta backing my petition. No judge would have given that sweet little girl to a guy like me . . . not with my history with women.'

'Tell me what you want from me.'

'Reese, you married Marie after she had been an Indian captive. I know the poor gal served as a wife to Big Nose, that small-time Indian chief over in Canada. Considering all of the obstacles she and you had to overcome, I figured you would be the one man to advise me about my situation.'

'Be careful, boy,' Reese warned. 'I'm beginning to think you might actually have true feelings for this nanny of yours.'

Cliff heaved another deep sigh. 'She's all I can think about, night and day, without rest, even when I'm trying to concentrate on something else. I've never been affected like this before, not by any girl or woman I ever met.'

'And her words were that you *didn't know the truth about her*?'

'Yeah,' Cliff replied. 'I mean, how bad could a girl's history be when she's never been out on her own and isn't yet eighteen?'

Reese studied Cliff for a time. The man had never been sincere when it came to women. He was a skirt-chasing tomcat, without morals or conscience. But he appeared completely honest and truthful at the moment. He actually seemed as lost as Reese had always felt around the opposite sex. It was the reason he and Marie were so well suited – her suffering from feelings of disgrace, and him drowning in feelings of awkwardness and uncertainty. Their relationship was like a gift from the Lord, Him bringing the two of them together like two lost yet matching bookends.

'Marie is supposed to get together with Mom to plan Wendy's birthday gathering that's coming up.' He grunted. 'Liable to be Wendy and July's announcement of their engagement too.' He went on. 'I'll ask her if she will speak to Mikki. Might be that a woman who had to overcome one of the most horrific existences a person can imagine would be able to get a troubled girl to confide in her.'

'That would be . . .'

Reese raised his hand to stop him from continuing. 'However,' he said gravely, 'if she tells Marie something in strict confidence, it will be up to Marie as to how much we can tell you. This isn't a mission to spy on the nanny.'

'I understand,' Cliff said. 'All I want is to know how I can make the situation better, and I can't do that until I know what her problem is.'

'All right, I'll do what I can, but this is all up to Marie. We've both been trying to put her past behind her. Her speaking of her own terrible memories – well, I hate to think of how many nightmares it will cause. She's barely sleeping through the night now.'

'I wouldn't ask if I didn't have such strong feelings about this girl.'

Reese bobbed his head. 'One thing. . . .' Once he had Cliff's undivided attention, he said: 'If you hurt this young lady, I'll make sure Jared hears about it.'

Cliff swallowed hard. 'Yeah . . . OK.'

'You know what he'll do to you?'

Cliff managed to nod. 'He'll kill me.'

'Only if he takes pity on you,' Reese said. Then he grinned. 'So long as you're clear on the possible consequences, do you still want me to have Marie talk to the nanny?'

Straightening himself more erect in the saddle, Cliff nodded a second time. 'Yes, I do, Reese. I promise you, I won't do this girl dirt.'

'Congratulations, cousin!' Reese laughed. 'I think the love bug has bitten you big time.'

Jared met Brett when he arrived by train. The two of them shook hands and then got together with Sergeant Fielding for a meal. After Brett explained all he'd done concerning the ship captain and the contracted laborers, they filled him in about Faro and the undercover policeman.

'I have to tell you,' Brett said, as the meal progressed. 'I never had so many people thanking me and claiming they would keep me in their prayers. It was like being a Christmas spirit and bringing joy and happiness to every one of them.'

'I'll bet,' Fielding said. 'You gave them back five years of their lives.'

Brett chuckled. 'More than that, Bryles and me staked them each to the thirty-eight dollars the captain was to receive in payment for them. As nothing could really be proved against the captain, other than promoting questionable contracts, we figured it was a satisfactory fine. Take him a good many months to earn back the money he lost.'

'Are you going home for a visit, or sticking around until Faro and Munson report on their findings?'

'I've got to get back, Jer. This has been the longest job of my life, being away from Desiree, the baby, and home. The last time I helped out it was only a few days. With all of this travel . . .'

Jared stopped his explanation. 'We are in complete agreement with you, Brett. You catch the next train to Cheyenne. Wyatt is standing by at the ranch. He can bring whatever help we might need.'

'With my department being involved, our people will probably handle most of this,' Fielding spoke up. 'I mean we do occasionally function on our own without Valeron help or influence.'

The three of them laughed.

The man who stormed into the sheriff's office was unknown to Desiree. The part-time deputy was asleep, having been called out during the night to settle a fight at the saloon. Leaving the baby with Wendy and July, Desiree occasionally filled in for Brett when needed. She felt perfectly safe in the town of Valeron, but she had also worked for the Pinkerton agency. It prompted her to maintain a certain caution when confronted by anyone she didn't know. She slipped her small Remington Double Derringer from the desk drawer and placed it onto her lap, keeping it hidden from the stranger. Remaining seated, she studied the imposing, angry looking brute that marched up to her desk.

'Can I help you with something?' she asked him politely.

He was a large, hirsute man, with thick hair showing from his knuckles to where his rolled-up cotton shirt hid his upper arms, and the same coarse black hair was visible from his open collar right up to his trim beard. Dressed in an expensive suit and polished shoes, he looked to be a businessman of sorts. Despite his bulky frame, he had a hawkish face, with a pointed chin and beaked nose that nearly reached his upper lip. He squinted his frigid black eyes from the darker interior of being inside a building and quickly scanned the room.

'Where's the sheriff?'

It was more a demand than a question, but Desiree remained civil. 'My husband is due back today or tomorrow; I'm watching the office at the moment.'

'I've come to see Nessy Mason,' he announced in an equally demanding voice.

Desiree did not hide her shock. 'Nessy?'

He pulled out a copy of the Denver newspaper. 'This here story about her hiring a nanny,' he growled. 'I'm durn-near certain the nanny mentioned belongs to me.'

Desiree immediately regretted the follow-up story that had appeared about how the eight-year-old had placed an ad in the local paper and hired herself a nanny. Somehow, it had made its way into the Denver paper… no doubt, a human interest story.

'Who, may I ask, are you?'

He scowled at her. 'I'm the one doing the asking here. My house girl ran off and I aim to get her back!'

'Are you wanting the sheriff to look into your claim?'

With a menacing step forward, he thrust out his jaw and sneered: 'I can find her on my own! Just tell me where this

Nessy Mason lives.'

Unmoved by his belligerence, Desiree responded with a calm demeanor. 'Before I provide you with any information, first tell me your name and how this nanny person might *belong* to you.'

Aggressively, he bent at the waist and banged both fists down on the desktop. 'I don't have to tell you nothing, woman! Answer the damn question!'

Desiree snapped the gun up and aligned it right between his eyes. He jerked upright, the rage immediately transformed into shock.

'Now, now,' she warned him in a very calm, yet icy tone of voice. 'You don't want to threaten a lawman's wife. That would leave you either dead on the floor or sitting behind bars until my husband returns . . . at which time, he would beat you until you didn't know your own name!'

Slowly, the man lifted his hands and stepped away from the desk. 'I reckon I lost my temper, ma'am,' he said without the slightest hostility. 'This girl is real important to me. I've been worried sick that something bad might have happened to her.'

'She ran away from you,' Desiree voiced her own opinion. 'That suggests she doesn't wish to *belong* to you.'

The man swallowed his bile and took on a more sincere appeal. 'We had a bit of a fight – more of a misunderstanding really – and she run off.'

'Perhaps if you were to allow your... house girl,' she added meaningfully, 'a few days to come to her senses?'

'It's been a few days already,' he countered. 'I admit I've a bit of a temper, but I intend to make her my wife. I want her back.'

'She seemed quite young.'

'Fifteen,' he said, 'though I think she's been lying about her age since I took her in.'

'And you're what . . . thirty-something?'

He was immediately rankled. 'Like I said, the girl's gonna be my wife. If I have to get a judge to back up my claim, I can do it.'

Desiree leaned back in her chair, still holding the gun on him. 'What is your name?'

'Elmer Baddon.'

'Well, Mr Baddon, I am not going to tell you where to find this nanny. Unless you can produce a court order, you will have to wait until my husband returns. He will deal with your claim and take you to her if he so decides.'

'Why'n hell . . .' he corrected the profanity. 'I mean why should I have to sit around and wait for your husband? All I want is to talk to the runaway!'

'I've given you the choices available, Mr Baddon: court order, or wait for my husband. I received a wire this morning saying he was on his way home. That should be sometime tomorrow.'

'Never mind,' he said gruffly. 'I'll take care of this on my own.'

'Mr Baddon,' she warned him. 'If you threaten anyone in town while trying to locate the nanny, I will lock you up.'

He snorted his disdain. 'You and who else?'

She displayed a placid smile. 'We have a deputy available. Plus, my married name is Valeron. I'm sure you noticed this town is named after my husband's family. It would take but a single word or wave of my hand, and

88

twenty armed men will be standing by, ready to do my bidding. Do you really want to get on my bad side?'

If the man had had false teeth, he might have swallowed them. 'No,' he muttered apologetically. 'No, Mrs Valeron. I'll be back with a court order.'

'Fine,' she said. 'See you then.'

Faro and Munson began their mine inspection when the morning shift arrived. The general foreman, Benny Janks, took them on a tour. He was knowledgeable and drew a good wage. As for the quality of miners, he explained how only a few experienced men had actually been hired. Many of them were working off prison sentences, while the majority were contracted immigrant laborers. The difference between the class of workers was obvious. Faro spoke to and selected one or two men from each group and made an appointment to speak to them. Janks was worried that Gaskell would not be happy about it, but Faro insisted it was all part of the inspection process.

Once they were back at the surface, Munson handed the list of names to Janks.

'These are the men and times for their short interviews,' Faro informed him. 'Have each of those men over at our hotel room at the appointed hour.'

'Going to mess with my schedule all day,' Janks complained. 'I don't agree with some of the rules here, but I am well paid to get the desired results.'

'Meaning what?' Faro asked.

'We have a certain number of ore cars that must be filled each week,' Janks outlined. 'If it takes working sixteen hours a day, seven days a week, that's what we do to meet the quota. I'll tell you one thing, I don't never not make the quota.'

'Sounds like a slavery operation,' Faro suggested.

'That's why I keep the men working hard. So long as we are done by Saturday night, everyone gets Sunday off. The miners know the rules, so most of them bust their backs to see we fill those rail cars on time.'

'The interviews won't take but a few minutes for each man.'

Janks bobbed his head. 'Then I'll do my best to get them there on time. We're battling through some rock that's tough as railroad spikes right now. I've got a second team working a new shaft, but it takes time to reach a zone with enough color to show a respectable yield.'

Faro frowned his concern. 'I can issue an order to stop all work for a half-day or so. That way, you'd have time to catch up. Would you prefer that?'

Janks, who chewed tobacco incessantly, nearly swallowed his chaw. 'It wouldn't make no difference. We would still have to fill the set number of rail cars.' He shrugged. 'Don't like working nights to make the quota, but that's what we would end up doing.'

'Then I will expect you to have the men on this list at my room – that's room number ten – at the appointed times. There are only six men and the interviews will take no longer than ten to fifteen minutes each. I'll try and push them through quickly. Is that satisfactory?'

'Yeah, that's fine.'

'OK.' Faro ended that part of the request. 'As soon as we are finished, I will make a list of my conclusions. Could you set up a meeting with Mr Gaskell at three this afternoon to go over our findings?'

'Uh, I'll give it a try, but Mr Gaskell don't exactly take orders − he's the one who gives them.'

'I'm sure he will make himself available for us. We don't wish to be a burden to your mining operation any longer than necessary.'

'I'll let Drummer know so he can set things up with the boss.'

Faro stuck out his hand. 'It's been a pleasure meeting you, Benjamin Janks.'

'Likewise,' Janks replied.

Once left alone, Munson grinned at Faro. 'You might not be a real government official, but you sure enough got the mannerism down pat.'

Faro chuckled. 'If you ever play cards with some of my family, you'll understand one fact − the only thing we do better than bluff is to get results.'

Wendy arrived to discover Nessy playing with Lana's oldest girl and Martin's oldest boy. Wanetta was watching them rather than the nanny.

'Hey, Mom!' Wendy greeted her. 'Where's the hired help?'

Wanetta waved her over to where she was sitting on one of the porch chairs. As soon as Wendy sat down next to her, Wanetta spoke to her in a quiet voice. 'Marie is having a heart-to-heart with Mikki.'

'Yeah? About what?'

Wanetta sighed. 'It's such a drama around here lately, like one of those traveling theater shows. Cliff wants to court Mikki, but Mikki is hiding something from him. Cliff spoke to Reese and Reese spoke to Marie. Due to Marie's gruesome history, she is talking to Mikki. I mean, who could have had a much worse life than Marie?' She frowned after finishing and asked, 'Now, dear daughter, what brings you out here in the middle of the week? Your birthday party is still two weeks away.'

'More drama, I'm afraid.' She told her about the man who had confronted Desiree.

Before they could enter the house and interrupt the meeting inside, Marie came out the door.

'Hi, Wendy!' she said, beaming her a bright smile. 'What are you doing here?'

Wendy explained a second time. Marie's complexion darkened and her mood changed from a warm greeting to an obvious internal fury. The expression caused Wendy to rise up out of her chair.

'Heavens!' she exclaimed. 'Whatever did I say?'

'Elmer Baddon!' Marie bit the name off as if it was vile or dirty. 'That's the man she told me about, the one she ran away from.'

'Excuse me,' Wanetta interrupted. 'But I'm completely in the dark here. Who's Elmer and what's this about running away?'

Marie took hold of both of the other women's hands and led them around to the far side of the house. She stopped a good thirty feet from the structure so no one nearby or in the house would overhear what was being said. Then she heaved a deep sigh.

'It took a lot of coaxing, and no little confessing my own life of shame and degradation, but Mikki finally told me why she had run away. If my eyes are red, it's because we both did our share of crying.'

'So give!' Wendy showed impatience. 'No telling when this guy might show up. If he has learned Mikki's here, he could ride in at any minute.'

Marie explained what she'd been told. 'Elmer took in Mikki when she was orphaned at ten years of age. He hired her out to anyone who needed a child tended or do cleaning, pull weeds, paint a fence ... anything. Mikki finally ended up with a job overseeing a neighboring family with four children.'

'She mentioned that family,' Wanetta put in.

'Yes, but she didn't mention that Elmer has had his hands all over her since she turned twelve! That filthy animal has only been waiting until she turned sixteen so he could marry her. If she hadn't lied to him about her age, he would be her husband!'

'The dirty, stinking, maggot!' Wanetta cried. 'I wish Desiree would have shot him on the spot!'

'She couldn't have known what a walking bucket of filth this guy is,' Wendy defended Desiree. 'He told her they'd had a simple quarrel.'

'No surprise the lowlife pervert would lie about his relationship,' Wanetta said. 'What are our options?'

'He's not taking her back!' Wendy declared vehemently. 'If I have to tell Jared about that child molester, I'll darn well do it!'

'It is tempting,' Wanetta agreed. 'Jared would give him what anyone who harms a child deserves.'

'Wyatt's here, isn't he?' Wendy asked. 'We should get word to him.'

'He's off with your father for the day. The two of them

went over to visit Troy.'

'We ought to get Mikki's input first,' Marie said. 'After all, she's the one who has to make a decision. If she wants to remain free, we'll see to it that she stays right here with us. If, however, she opts to speak to the walking dung-heap, perhaps talk things through. . . .'

'You don't talk to child molesters!' Wendy avowed. 'Those inhuman beasts deserve nothing more than a public hanging!'

Wanetta smiled. 'Spoken exactly like your brother.'

'Yes, Mother, because there is nothing worse than a man who takes advantage of a child – especially when that child is in his care!'

'Mikki told me her story in confidence,' Marie explained to the other two women. 'I confided in you. That means you can't repeat anything I've told you. Mikki doesn't wish to be pitied or questioned about her past. I promised not to tell anyone what we had talked about, meaning I'm breaking my word talking to you both.' Marie shook her head. 'Of course, that was before some vermin showed up who wants to try and claim her.'

'We will keep this between the three of us,' Wanetta said. 'If the man makes a nuisance of himself, we may have to involve one of the family.'

'Jared,' Wendy mouthed his name almost reverently.

Her mother shook her head. 'Not yet. Wyatt will see no one takes the girl against her wishes . . . unless we have to deal with a court order.'

'Whatever else happens,' Marie said, 'I don't want that young lady to ever have to face Elmer again.'

'Have Reese send Cliff back to the house,' Wanetta told

Marie. Then she looked at Wendy. 'Your father and Wyatt will be home by dark. Until this is settled, I want a man here at all times.'

CHAPTER SEVEN

From behind his desk, Ward Gaskell welcomed the two mine inspectors with a grunt. He didn't offer a handshake, but nodded at the two vacant chairs opposite of him.

'My name is Faro, and this is my assistant, Mr Munson,' Valeron introduced. 'I am bound by duty of my office to make certain recommendations concerning your mining operation.'

'Speak your piece,' Gaskell said, pausing to light an expensive-looking cigar. He sucked in air until the tip glowed, then purposely blew the smoke in the direction of Faro and Munson.

Faro ignored the contemptuous act and opened a notebook. Glancing at the page, he began with a few statistics.

'Over a dozen deaths this past year – three of them assigned prisoners, working off non-violent offenses. At least two public floggings – which is illegal – and more than twenty contracted employees hospitalized at your private infirmary, including several children.' He flipped the page. 'A number of beatings, several women who claim they have been forced to work in your saloons. . . .'

'I thought you were a safety inspector for the mine!' Gaskell disrupted his string of claims.

Faro lifted his chin piously and finished his statement. 'Plus, many of the contracted children are forced to work twelve- to fourteen-hour shifts.'

'You can speak to Judge Sayles if you wish,' the man dismissed the complaint. 'Colorado has no labor laws regarding children.'

'The "judge", as you call him, was appointed by you,' Munson interjected. 'His only credentials are that he was a lawyer.'

Gaskell frowned. 'You two are mighty nosy for simple mine inspectors.'

'Humane treatment is understood within the Colorado judicial system, Mr Gaskell,' Munson countered. 'Slave labor in any form is not tolerated at either the state or federal level.'

Gaskell snorted his disdain. 'All right, fellows. What is it going to cost me to be rid of you and any further state interference?'

'Be careful of what you say,' Faro warned. 'It is a crime to attempt to bribe a state official.'

'Bribe, donate, support . . .' he shrugged. 'It always comes down to money.'

'After visiting your cemetery, I could not help but notice the name of Decker on several of the grave markers.'

'Syrus Decker was a little too ambitious when it came to discipline, but he was shot and killed a short time back. I've a new man in charge who isn't so enthusiastic.'

'The mine needs more support beams in many areas,

along with a second vent shaft to the center of your diggings. I also noticed many of your people are working with poor tools and using rags for gloves.'

'I'll look into that,' Gaskell said. 'But this is a private company. The state has no right to come in and dictate how I run my organization.'

'On the contrary,' Munson argued. 'You are using state, city and county prisoners in your mines. Those men are under the state's control and protection. If they are not being treated fairly, we will have them removed from your service.'

The man's teeth clamped down on his cigar with barely controlled vigor, his color darkening as he reined in his anger. 'Like I said, I'll see about making more gloves and some better tools available.'

'As for the children . . .' Faro began.

Gaskell waved a hand to dismiss the complaint. 'I'll speak to the overseer and have him reduce their hours to no more than ten a day.'

'What about schooling or education? When these contracts are up, the children and people need to be prepared to enter society and earn a living.'

'I offer them a job right here with fair wages and housing,' the company owner said. 'Can't say I'm not doing my part.'

'You won't mind if we send someone to supervise the improvements . . . say in a couple of weeks?'

'As long as he pays for his keep. We run an open company here and operate the town like any other. Feel free to come back and spend as long as you like.'

'Very good,' Faro said. 'We will be going now.'

Gaskell didn't offer a goodbye or his hand. He simply blew another puff of smoke in their direction and returned to working on some papers on his desk.

Reese spoke to Cliff, giving him what little he could from what Marie had passed along. Even then, he made Cliff promise to keep every word of it private. He explained Mikki's situation was dire due to the arrival of Elmer. As he feared, Cliff was furious.

'You're saying that guy mistreated her, that he hurt her!' Cliff swore vehemently. 'If he shows up, I'll put a bullet in his fat gut!'

'He claimed he would get a decree from a judge. We would first have to get that overturned. If we could prove he had been mistreating the child. . . .'

'What proof?' Cliff cried. 'You said Mikki confided in Marie, but she isn't going to want to stand in front of a judge and tell him every detail about how Elmer harmed her! Besides, it would be the word of a runaway against the man who has been her accepted guardian for the last few years.'

'Let the family handle this, Cliff. You stand by Mikki, comfort and support her in whatever way you can, but let us handle Elmer. Martin knows enough about law to give us grounds to keep Mikki safe on the ranch. Then we will decide how to handle Elmer if he pushes this.'

Cliff was swayed by Reese's logic. He swallowed his ire and gave a nod of consent. 'All right, we'll try it your way. But if this guy manages to convince a judge to grant him custody. . . .'

'Trust me,' Reese promised. 'We'll handle Mr Baddon.'

'Damn, Reese,' Cliff groaned. 'How come I keep ending up involved with girls in trouble?'

'Payback!' Reese declared. 'You've used girls all your life. It's time they used you for a change.'

'Thanks, cousin,' Cliff said dryly. 'It's nice to know whose side you're on!'

Jared was happy for the company when Shane arrived in Denver. As his room had two bunks, he paid for a second guest. After tossing Shane's gear in the room, the two of them went to a restaurant they both liked from their previous trip to the big city. After they ordered their meals, Jared filled him in on all that was taking place. In return, Shane shared what he had learned from Desiree when he caught the stage for Cheyenne.

'So some guy is claiming to be Mikki's guardian and to-be-husband, with legal hold over her?'

'I think there's more to it than that, but Desiree didn't know much. She was worried enough that she sent Wendy to the ranch to warn them about the guy. You know Desiree isn't the kind of gal to spook easily.'

'Brett should be back in Valeron by this time. I'm sure he can handle whatever is going on.'

'I hope so,' Shane said, still showing a worried mien. 'But Brett's hands are tied if this guy has the law on his side.'

'Soon as we get this settled, we'll have a talk with Reese or Cliff. They both know better than to try and dodge my questions. If there's something going on that Brett can't handle legally. . . .'

Shane didn't push him to complete the threat. Instead,

he turned to the lighter side of the story.

'You wouldn't believe Cliff. He's like a run-over snake in the road, tied up in knots until he can't think straight. He's fallen under the gal's spell, but she is keeping him at arm's length.'

'Good for Mikki. Cliff could stand to have his ego cut down a notch or two.'

Shane heaved a sigh. 'Tell you one thing, I'm sorry we're missing out on all of the fun and mystery at the ranch. I mean, if Cliff can't win a gal's favor. . . .'

'Yeah, that's something I'd like to see.'

The meal was served and the two began to eat. Shane gave an 'um' as he tasted the veal he had ordered. 'Sure like to take this recipe home for Mom to try.'

'Gwen is a darn good cook,' Jared praised his aunt. 'If you're not satisfied, you had better start looking for some gal who cooks or bakes for a living.'

Shane laughed shortly and turned to business. 'OK, so Wyatt is at the ranch, Brett went home and Faro won't be any help if we get into trouble. Are we counting on Fielding and the local lawmen to deal with whatever comes up?'

'There's only so much the law can do. According to Brett, these contracts are written without any buyout or exit clause. That's what makes them more of an indenture than a contract – and that's illegal.'

'What can we do?'

'Brett got the government involved back east and terminated all of the contracts of those people who just arrived in the country. We might only need to push the owner of Paradise to alter the contracts or something.'

'And if he won't?' Shane wanted to know.

'That's what Fielding will have to decide.'

'Come on, Jer, we're not going to let this guy get away with running a slave camp.'

'No, even prisoners serving time deserve a degree of humane treatment. That's part of what we can use against the mine owner. As for the individuals under contracts, those pieces of paper should be deemed illegal, due to being a form of indenture. If need be, we can threaten to cancel every one of those.' He grinned. 'We take his prisoners and contracted laborers – what's the guy got left?'

'A bunch of furious gunmen?'

Jared chuckled. 'If it comes to that, we've got Wyatt to join us, along with however many men Fielding can muster. I don't see a mine owner wanting an actual war.'

'You said Paradise is a big place. How many gunmen or toughs are up there, a couple dozen? Fifty or more?'

'Faro will have a count,' he replied. 'And Munson is an experienced lawman, though new to these parts. I reckon they will provide us with the information we need.'

'It's great to have such confidence, Jer,' Shane said. 'Wish you could give me a bowl full of it – I'd lick the dish clean in two seconds flat!'

The three riders entered the massive Valeron yard – three large houses, a barn that covered a quarter-acre, corrals and sheds, along with several bunkhouses. The milk cows were visible in a nearby field, with draft horses, goats, chickens and a few pigs nearby. One man was busy at a forge, working on new horseshoes, while a couple of dogs barked to announce the arrival of strangers.

The trio stopped their rental horses at the largest of the three houses. Cliff walked out to meet him, along with Locke Valeron.

'Don't bother to get down,' was Locke's greeting. 'If one of you is Elmer Baddon, you are not welcome on Valeron land.'

'I'm Baddon!' A bearded man spoke as he withdrew a paper from the inside of his shirt. 'I've got me a court order!' He ventured forth testily. 'This here paper gives me the right to take back the property what is rightfully mine.'

Locke turned to Cliff. 'Fetch Martin so he can look over the claim. He and Wyatt are over at their folks.'

Cliff glowered at Elmer, the urge to beat him with his fists so strong he could barely contain himself. Reese hadn't been able to tell him the whole truth, but before him was a man who had severely mistreated Mikki.

Locke gave him a gentle push with one hand. 'G'wan, son,' he coaxed. 'I told you, we will handle this lawfully.'

Cliff hurried over to Udall and Faye's house. Wyatt had already been alerted by the dogs. He and Martin were in the process of putting on their hats. Wyatt, as usual, also wore his gun. As the three of them approached Locke's house, the miner was making a fuss.

'I asked you where's my girl is?' Elmer shouted his demand. 'You try and keep her from me and I'll tear this place apart!'

'Don't let your mouth make promises that your body will regret,' Wyatt spoke up, causing the three men to all look in his direction.

'I got me a legal paper here,' Elmer snarled. 'Gimme

my property!'

Martin walked up to the man and stretched out his hand. 'May I?' he asked, always polite in his dealings.

Elmer shoved the document into his hand and Martin looked it over. After studying it for a moment he asked: 'Who is Judge Marisol?'

'He's a judge from Denver.'

'Says here he resides in Cherry Creek.'

'That's part of Denver.'

'It also lists his credentials as Justice of the Peace, not a recognized judgeship.'

'Judge . . . smudge,' one of the men with Elmer growled. 'What's the difference?'

Martin shook his head. 'The difference, my ignorant friend, is that this document has no validity.'

'Valid-what?'

'You need an order by a federal judge to procure an underage juvenile from out of state.'

'What do you mean by out of state?' Elmer cried.

'This ranch sits on the Wyoming side of the border. Did you not notice when you passed through town? Valeron is located on the Colorado-Wyoming border. Much of our holdings are on the Colorado side, but the ranch and half of the town are in Wyoming.'

'The hell with this!' Elmer bellowed, starting to dismount. 'I'm gonna take what's mine, right here, right now!'

But Wyatt's gun appeared magically, cocked and pointed at the man's head. 'If your foot touches our yard,' he warned Elmer in a voice hedged with frost, 'I'll splatter your brains all over your two pals.'

Martin moved up a step and handed him back the paper. 'Tell your friend, relative or whomever wrote out this worthless paper that a fraudulent act – that of supplying legal documents – could land him in court for exceeding his authority.'

'I'll be back with the army if need be!' Elmer threatened.

'Give Colonel Warring at the fort my regards when you make the request,' Locke told him causally. 'He and I share a committee on army-civilian affairs.'

Elmer yanked his horse's head with the bridle cruelly, and the three men whirled about and galloped out of the yard.

'That won't be the end of it,' Cliff said. 'He will be back.'

'We'll stop him,' Martin said. 'I can represent Miss Bruckner in court. If need be, I'll go before a judge and file a motion to have her assigned to our care. She is not yet of legal age, so it would be a form of guardianship.'

'Wendy wouldn't tell me everything,' Cliff told the three men. 'But she did claim the man mistreated her. She has been his personal slave since she was ten years old.'

'Wanetta was equally vague,' Locke admitted. 'She has never kept a secret from me that I know of, but she avowed this was not her secret to tell. Evidently, Marie had a heart-to-heart with the nanny. She kept most of the conversation to herself, but Wanetta did say one thing. . . .' He displayed a grave expression. 'If bad went to worse, they would let Wendy tell Jared the whole truth.'

Wyatt grunted. 'We all know what that means. Jared has always been the self-proclaimed protector of the women

105

on the Valeron ranch.'

'Yeah,' Cliff agreed. 'Jerry considers them to be lambs in his care.'

Locke sighed with finality. 'And woe be unto the man who dares harm one of his flock.'

Faro waved farewell to Jared and Shane as he boarded the train for Cheyenne. Munson was busy delivering his report to Fielding, so the two Valerons wandered over to see what conclusions or actions would come from the mine inspection sham. They arrived at the police station as Fielding was exiting the building.

'Just in time, boys,' Sergeant Fielding said. 'I'm on my way over to talk to Judge Burke. He's the judge who oversaw Trina Barrett's case and provided the warrants to arrest all those involved in the rustling ring you two brought down.'

'Think he can do anything about this?' Jared asked. 'I mean, this is a corporation, not an actual township. Does he have authority over something like this?'

'Burke is a sitting judge for Denver, but he also has federal authority. Brett used that angle to shut down the indenture scam being used by the ship captain.'

'I get it. If this can be deemed a slavery enterprise. . . ?' Jared posited.

'That's it, exactly,' Fielding responded. 'Plus, there are also the deaths of several prisoners to consider. Those men were under state, county or local city authority, meaning their safekeeping was in the hands of those wardens or superintendents. Each and every death should have been investigated.'

106

'Sounds like you've lined up a pretty good line of offenses.'

'I have a couple of the contracts Brett brought back with him. I've never seen one of the old indentures from back before the war, but these certainly look like a pledge of unwavering servitude to me.'

The three of them made their way up the street. Jared, ever watchful, spotted the man Wyatt claimed had been watching his every move. Without looking directly at him, he mentioned the spook to Fielding.

'Ronnie Cogg,' the lawman said, without needing to take a look. 'If I was a betting man, I would lay odds he and his pals are the ones who made Adams disappear – the runaway miner who first brought these contracts to our attention.'

'No proof against him?'

Fielding shrugged. 'No body. We did a pretty wide search, but there are a great many hiding places out in the nearby hills. More than a few empty holes or shafts where mining was attempted too. I suspect Adams is in a deep pit or buried under several feet of dirt.'

'Sounds like someone ought to be watching this Ronnie character,' Shane suggested.

'It's like trying to follow of gust of wind. The man knows all the tricks to prevent anyone from dogging his trail. Plus, he has two chums that work with him.'

Jared frowned. 'Maybe you haven't tried the direct approach.'

'Oh, we've talked to him a number of times. We interviewed him and his friends about Adams and harassment of other witnesses concerning a couple of deaths out at

Paradise, but nothing came of it. It's well known that Gaskell has the money and power to shut up anyone who intends to speak out against Paradise or him,'

'But you have no proof Ronnie has done any of that,' Shane deduced.

'His unsavory friends are a half-breed named Shade and a weasel of a gunman called Donner. We've never been able to pin anything on any of them. They are real good at covering each other's backs.'

'You think they might try and influence Judge Burke?' Jared wanted to know.

'I would guess that he and my captain are the two men in Denver they would never test. One wrong word or threat and they would end up behind bars.'

'Any chance they would try to dry-gulch Jer and me?' Shane asked, not hiding his concern. 'I mean if they figure out we're trying to bring down the king of Paradise. . . .'

He didn't have to finish, and Fielding's expression was not comforting. 'I can't say you two aren't riding on a slippery road,' he said carefully. 'But then, you came to us with this problem and now we're all involved.'

'Excuse me,' Shane reminded him. 'Wyatt is the one who came to you.' Then he added, 'And he's safely back at the ranch!'

Cliff stuck close to the house while Wyatt conferred with Martin and then went into Valeron to send off a couple dispatches to keep Jared informed and get input from Judge Burke in Denver. Locke and Wanetta went over to visit with other members of the family to finish planning the upcoming birthday party for Wendy. It left Cliff alone with Nessy and the nanny.

The night wore on and bedtime came for Cliff's little girl. He gave her a kiss and hug, told her how very special she was, then allowed Mikki to put her to bed. A few minutes later, Mikki came into the sitting room and took a seat in an easy chair across from where he was sitting. After a moment, she spoke up in a hushed voice.

'Nessy has told me how you rescued her from the tragic accident that took a nun's life.'

'Poor little tyke,' Cliff replied. 'She actually stuck a long stick out the back of the wagon like a gun, fearful the bad men had come back. She was trying to protect "Mam", as she called the lady.'

'It was very good of you to adopt her, especially with all of the other Valerons here. I would think a number of them would have been willing to do that.'

'Nessy took it in her head that I was her protector.' He smiled at the memory. 'She even attacked a full-grown man during a fight trying to protect me.'

'Yes, Scarlet told me the story about you and her in the bandit stronghold. She seemed to think you changed when Nessy came into your life.'

'Nothing makes a man grow up faster than taking on the responsibility of being a father. I had a change of heart about a good many things.'

Mikki ducked her head, seeming embarrassed. 'I . . . I wouldn't want anyone in your family to be hurt on my account.'

'Just like Nessy,' Cliff told her firmly, 'your life is worth fighting for. Elmer will never touch you again – I swear it on my own life.'

Her eyes lifted, filled with a mixture of compassion and wonder. 'But you hardly know me. I'm a stranger to you and your whole family.'

'You're Nessy's nanny,' he countered steadfastly. 'And you are part of this family . . . my family.'

'You can't mean that!' she said with some force. 'One of your kin could be hurt or killed by defying Elmer. He can hire a lot of men – tough, roughneck, dangerous men.'

Cliff chuckled. 'Maybe you haven't taken a close look at the Valeron family. Jared, Wyatt and Brett are all first rate men with a gun. Reese, Troy, Faro . . . every man sired by Locke, Temple and Udall. These are men of the west, men who have fought rustlers and Indians, the harsh weather and everything nature throws at us. But, foremost, these are devout men of honor and decency. They will always take up a fight on behalf of the weak or innocent. It's who they are.'

'And you, Cliff Mason,' she turned the arrow to point at him. 'Why are you so dead-set on defending me?'

'Ever since I set eyes on you, I knew you were something special.' Cliff saw her eyes grow a bit wider. 'I saw in you everything a man could want.' Mikki's lips parted, but no words came forth. Cliff continued to praise her. 'In you, young lady, I believe I've found something that has been lacking in my life for a long time.'

As the girl's head turned slightly from side to side, Cliff knew he had her on a romantic track. To lighten the moment, he finished: 'You are a perfect choice to be Nessy's nanny.'

Mikki frowned . . . then her features grew soft and she

laughed. It was a very pleasing laugh.

'I expected something a bit more personal from you. Tish, Marie, Wanetta – they all warned me of your boyish charm and ease around women.'

Cliff leaned back in his chair and smiled. 'I keep telling everyone I've changed.'

With a timid nod, 'Yes. And for the better. I remember.'

'I won't say I don't find the idea of courting you very tempting, Mikki, but you are young in both years and experience. I don't want to rush you into anything.'

The odd look crossed her face again, the one he had seen the last time she ran from the room. 'I . . . I have some adjusting to do too. I told you before that I couldn't. . . .' But a constriction stopped her flow of words.

Cliff lifted both of his hands. 'I'm not asking for any dark confessions, Mikki,' he said gently. 'I've never been patient when it came to courting a girl, but I am willing to be patient with you.' Displaying one of his most winning smiles, he added: 'I believe you are worth the wait.'

Mikki did not hide her relief, rising to her feet. 'Then I look forward to our getting to know one another better. Perhaps, down the road a way – if Elmer doesn't take me away – we can discuss a proper way to begin a courtship.'

Cliff also stood up. He moved over and took her hand. Holding it between his own, he gave her a short bow. 'I bid you goodnight, Mikki. And I again thank you for the care and tenderness you have shown my little girl.'

Mikki did not pull away. When he let go of her hand, she said goodnight and left him alone in the sitting room.

Cliff watched her leave and felt as if a part of his heart had walked out of the room with her. It was an odd sensation, yet he enjoyed it somehow.

CHAPTER EIGHT

Jane tapped lightly at the door and then opened it. Gaskell was relaxing in his comfortable, leather-bound chair, smoking a cigar.

'What is it?' he asked.

'Mr Cogg to see you,' Jane answered. 'He said you would want to speak to him.'

'Thank you, Miss Lawrence. You can let him come in.'

Ronnie walked through the door and then paused to turn his head and watch the secretary walk away. When he looked at Gaskell, a smirk curled his lips.

'Nothing but the best for the king of Paradise,' he said, walking over to sit down in the chair opposite Gaskell's desk. 'Fine lookin' filly, Ward.'

'What's happening, Ronnie?' Gaskell was concerned. 'You don't usually come all the way up here, not when a telegraph message will suffice.'

'This ain't something I wanted spread around, Ward.'

Gaskell crushed the smoke in an ashtray. 'Let me have it. What's going on?'

'After I sent the message to you to say Wyatt Valeron

had left town, I spotted a second Valeron hanging around – maybe two of them.

As Gaskell listened, Ronnie told him about the pair and how they had met up with Sergeant Fielding.

'But you said the Mackavoy family took the train for back east,' Gaskell said. 'And if Wyatt left town, what could be going on?'

'Them two that come up here – the mine inspectors Parker told me to watch for?' At Gaskell's nod, he continued. 'Well, only one of them left town. The other one – turns out he's a policeman. He arrived in Denver a few days before he joined up with that Faro character. Shade seen Faro talking to one of the new Valeron boys too. That means Fielding and the Valerons must have something up their sleeve.'

Gaskell pounded a doubled fist on the desktop. 'I knew them two were phonies! This is some kind of under-handed trick. The law and the Valerons are going to try and destroy everything I've built up!'

'Be my guess,' Ronnie concurred. 'One of the clerks who does office work at the police station told me Fielding had got hold of several contracts you use for hiring imported workers. He said they came from a batch of people who just arrived from England.'

'So that's why no new contracted employees have showed up. They should have been here several days ago. Van Stokes sent a message saying he was shipping over a dozen people and we've yet to see a single one.'

Ronnie rubbed the stubble along his jaw. 'Meaning someone must have shut down the operation at that end. This isn't good, Ward. This isn't good at all.'

'We've been working together since the war, Ronnie,' Gaskell told his friend. 'You never wanted the life out here, but you've been the most important man I have on the payroll.'

Ronnie chuckled. 'Don't lay it on too thick, Ward. You've always paid me top dollar for usually doing almost nothing.'

'Yes, but you took care of Adams. You've made sure the people released from here never told their story to the law. You've been a big part of our continued success.'

'Get to the part of how I can help this time, Ward.'

'Those two men – maybe both Valerons?' He snorted his contempt. 'They need to disappear.'

Ronnie tighten his brow, squinting from his pinched expression. 'Damn, Ward,' he whispered the words. 'They are working with Fielding. How are we going to do anything without bringing the law down on all of us?'

'I've got a few men we can use for the chore. Just make sure you and your two men are seen in town when it happens. If you have an alibi, no one can point a figure at us.'

'I reckon Drummer is the one to talk to,' Ronnie said, considering the job.

'Yes,' Gaskell agreed. 'We need to keep this within our control. No third party involved; we handle it ourselves.'

'I'll go discuss it with him.'

'Ronnie, I can't imagine why you never wanted to work alongside me. You've always had a quick mind.'

He grinned. 'I like my free time too much for that, Ward. The job I have gives me all the freedom I want. I don't aim to end up like you, sitting behind a desk and

115

worrying day and night.' Then he rolled his eyes and nodded in the direction of his secretary. 'Though I admit there does appear to be some special benefits up here.'

Gaskell winked. 'Man needs a little diversion from his work sometimes.'

'Diversion,' Ronnie chuckled. 'There's a word I like. Never was sure of the meaning, but when it comes to women…' He didn't have to finish.

'We have several pretty, consenting girls at the saloon, if you'd like to enjoy a little diversion before you leave.'

Ronnie laughed. 'I'll talk to Drummer first, then check out the fillies in your stable.'

Wendy and July Colby were doing the monthly report on the four businesses in Valeron that were family owned. It was a surprise to have Martin walk into the office.

'You're about three days early for the paperwork,' Wendy addressed her cousin. 'Is there a problem?'

Martin looked at Wendy's assistant and suitor. 'Can you give us a few minutes, July?'

'Sure thing, Martin,' he said. 'I'll walk down and rustle us up a pastry from the bakery. Want me to bring you something?'

Martin patted his slightly protruding stomach. 'Jean is threatening to cut down my meals if I don't get more exercise. Make mine something small.'

July left the office and Martin got right down to business.

'The nanny issue is coming to a head,' he told Wendy. 'We got a cable from Judge Burke in Denver. He said that while Judge Marisol didn't have jurisdiction in ordering us to give up the nanny from across the state line, Elmer has enough witnesses that he could get legal backing. There was never a formal guardianship or adoption, but the girl has been his ward for the last seven years. It's kind of like common-law marriages – when a man and a women reside together long enough, they are considered a couple.'

'But he has it in his head to marry the child he raised!' Wendy cried. 'Worse than that, he . . .' she struggled against her conscience, unable to break her vow of confidentiality. Instead, she told him, 'That man treated Mikki terribly, Martin. I mean it. Really, really terribly!'

Her cousin didn't need convincing. 'That's why I've come to town. I'll help July finish up this month's reports. As for you, Wyatt thinks you and he should go to Denver. When doing a background check on Elmer, a police department report listed a death that was linked to him a couple years back. No charges were ever made, but it might be worth looking into.'

'All right. I'll throw a few things together in a bag. Is Wyatt getting a buggy or are we going to wait for the stage?'

'He is over getting a carriage. He'll be here in a few minutes.'

Wendy sighed. 'I hope I'm back for my birthday party. There was something of importance I wanted to announce.'

Martin grinned. 'Yes, I see your *something of importance* headed this way. We'll let him know you'll be back in a few days and that I'll help finish up the reports.'

After speaking with Judge Burke, Fielding decided they

had enough evidence to confront Gaskell and insist he terminate all of the crooked contracts. He could offer those same people employment, but would no longer have a legal hold over them. As for the prisoners, all of them would be returned to their original situations. There would be no continued penal slave labor for him from this point forward.

Shane, Jared and Fielding picked up their horses and left the stable together. However, when they reached the outskirts of town, Jared disclosed he had a bad feeling. Fielding halted the expedition immediately and asked what it was. He knew Jared's hunter instincts were far superior to his own.

'It started yesterday,' Jared told him. 'Ronnie and his two pals stopped watching us like hawks. Even so, I did see one of them spying on us when we went to visit the judge.'

Fielding picked up on his logic. 'They have been doggin' our every move, yet they are suddenly ignoring us. That doesn't bode well for our trip to Paradise.'

'What are you two talking about?' Shane wanted to know. 'We no longer have a couple watchdogs. Isn't that a good thing?'

'It means they have decided on their next move, cuz,' Jared explained. 'Our leaving town isn't a surprise – it's what they expected.'

'You don't think they are going to be waiting for us along the trail?'

'Good chance,' Jared said.

'But,' Shane argued, 'Ronnie and his two pards were at the restaurant when we walked down to get our horses. We saw all three of them!'

'Yes,' Jared agreed, 'sitting right out in plain sight; didn't give us a second look.'

'Providing themselves with a solid alibi,' Fielding contributed. 'Exactly what they would do if they knew someone was going to set an ambush for us.'

'What'll we do?' Shane cried. 'We can't simply ride into a trap!'

Jared frowned in thought. After a moment, he said, 'We'll follow the main trail until we reach the foothills. Then you two sit tight for fifteen minutes while I slip away to scout ahead. Once the time is up, continue at an easy pace. They might have something planned, but it will likely be up the trail a piece. After all, they wouldn't ambush us where someone living near the city could hear the gunfire. I suspect they will make their attempt a respectable distance along the trail. It should give me time to locate the shooters before you get in range.'

'Should?' Shane yelped. 'It *should* give you time? What if it doesn't?'

'Then I'll be justified in killing every one of those dry-gulching rats.' He held a granite expression for several seconds and then grinned. 'Trust me, cuz. Have I ever got you killed yet?'

'Being strung up at the slaughterhouse, ready to be gutted, was pretty darn close!' Shane reminded him.

'Shucks, that was just a little added excitement. What good is a rescue if someone isn't in true peril?'

'I'd just as soon not have the extra excitement, Jer. See that you don't wait too long to start shooting. I'd as soon not end up with an ounce or two of lead in me.'

Jared glanced at Fielding. 'Sometimes I think the

119

youngest male offspring in a family gets short-changed on grit and vigor.'

'I wouldn't know,' the lawman said. 'I'm the only boy in my family. I can tell you, it's tough with three older sisters.'

'Shane got lucky there. Two of his three sisters are younger than him.'

'Durned if I don't miss having Cliff along,' Shane muttered. 'At least when he is around, I'm not the target for all of the teasing.'

Judge Burke was at his house. His wife answered the door and allowed Wendy and Wyatt to enter the man's den so they could speak in private.

'Nice to see you again, Judge Burke,' Wendy said cheerfully. 'Trina Barrett Valeron sends her regards.'

He grinned. 'As I recall, your brother did seem quite taken with her.'

'Yes, they have a medical clinic up at White Point.'

Turning his attention to Wyatt. 'And you, young man, have you rounded up another string of rapscallions for me to pass judgment on?'

He chuckled. 'I'm sure my cousins and the local law are working on that as we speak.'

'Yes, I looked over the contracts being used up at Paradise for Sergeant Fielding and two of your kinfolk yesterday.'

'We learned at the police station that they left this morning before we arrived,' Wyatt confirmed.

'Is this visit concerning the same crime?'

'Actually, we are here about a matter where no one was charged. My brother, Martin, contacted you a short time back about a man named Elmer Baddon. He is attempting to force a young girl into marriage, a girl who had previously been in his care . . . a Mikki Bruckner.'

'I remember.'

'It's this way,' Wendy took over. 'We know that Elmer took advantage of and mistreated Mikki, but we also know it's something very hard to prove.' The judge nodded his understanding of the circumstances, so she continued. 'However, we learned that another girl had been involved with Baddon some time back, a girl who took her own life.'

'Yes, Gina Lopez. It was very tragic,' Burke acknowledged. 'But I am not given to comment on previous cases . . . even when I was unhappy with the outcome. It isn't professional.'

'Maybe you could just give us a little general information,' Wendy coerced. 'I mean there must have been some conclusion as to why she committed suicide.'

He sighed. 'She was with child. Barely sixteen and unmarried, she did not wish to be ostracized by society. As I said, it was very tragic.'

'What was Elmer's role in her death?' Wyatt wanted to know. 'We need some kind of leverage to prevent Mikki from being returned to a man we know has treated her badly in the past.'

The judge was thoughtful for a moment. When he spoke, there was a grim determination in his expression. 'Gina was not very attractive and didn't have any male suitors. Elmer Baddon was known to have spent some time with her and even bought her gifts. It is suspected that he was the father of the child, but he refused to marry her.'

'So he drove her to suicide,' Wendy concluded.

121

'All circumstantial and undocumented,' Judge Burke declared. 'It's why no charges were filed concerning Gina's death.'

'We spoke to the dead girl's mother before coming to see you,' Wendy informed him. 'She claimed her work left Gina alone much of the time. Elmer took advantage of Gina being lonely, inexperienced and naive. He courted a girl who was not yet sixteen and left her in a family way.'

'Again,' Judge Burke said, 'many girls are married by the age of sixteen. And while it is certainly the honorable thing to do, there is no law declaring a man must marry a woman who claims to be carrying his child.'

'What if he was mistreating a child in his custody in the very same way?' Wendy asked testily. 'Is that not a crime?'

The judge's expression grew dark. 'Is that what Mikki is claiming? That Elmer forced her to have relations with him?'

Wendy struggled with her reply. 'I'm bound by a solemn promise not to answer that. It's more of a general question, rather than making a charge against anyone.'

'I know the police were called to the Baddon house on at least one occasion. A neighbor reported a girl crying when Elmer was home with Mikki. However, his explanation was satisfactory for the policeman and no charges were brought against him.'

Wyatt chose to speak up. 'What would be the chance of our family getting guardianship for the girl, so she would not have to be returned to his custody?'

'You live on the Wyoming side of the border,' Burke pointed out. 'And without proof of Elmer's mistreatment, I doubt any judge would make such a decree. After all, the girl has been in his care for several years.'

Wyatt looked at Wendy. 'It would appear we have no legal recourse, not unless Mikki testifies against Elmer. Even then, it would be her word against his.'

Wendy didn't argue. Instead, she gave a nod to the judge. 'We thank you kindly for your time. It's obvious the court will favor Mr Baddon's claim, but we had to try.'

'I'm sorry,' the judge replied. 'But the law is on his side. If I were to rule against him, my own position would be at risk. Without proof. . . ?' He raised his shoulders in a helpless gesture.

Wendy and Wyatt left the judge's house. Once on the walkway, Wyatt told his cousin, 'I want to stick around until Jerry and Sergeant Fielding return. They ought to be back by tomorrow. If you want, we can get you on the next train going to Cheyenne.'

'No, I'll wait with you. I want to make sure Shane and Jerry get back safely.'

'Then let's rent a couple rooms at the hotel and have something to eat. We've got a little time on our hands, so I'll let you shop around and pick out your own birthday present.'

She put on a sly grin. 'You might rue those words, cousin Wyatt. I have expensive tastes.'

'Yeah.' He laughed softly. 'But I expect you're worth it.'

Jared was glad he had brought his favorite hunting mare with him to Denver. Sprite moved through the trees and brush with the stealth of a mountain buck. Long on endurance, yet built for speed, the half-Morgan, half-Indian pony was a little smaller than a purebred Morgan.

What the mare lacked in size, she made up in stamina and heart. Plus, she had that extra sense, seemingly aware of when Jared needed her to be extra quiet or careful. More than once she had warned him of danger through the perking or flattening of her ears. With Sprite's keener hearing, Jared used her in the same manner as a grouse hunter used a well-trained bird dog.

Taking it slow and easy caused him precious minutes, but the caution paid off. Sprite's ears perked and she looked off toward a thick chaparral. Jared caught sight of three horses and stopped dead still.

Being downwind, the trio of saddled broncs did not react to their presence. He hushed Sprite and patted her on the neck.

'Good girl,' he whispered. 'You stay here and be real quiet.'

The horse did not even twitch her tail, standing alert, yet immobile, as Jared eased his rifle out of its sheath and quietly jacked a bullet into the chamber. Then, with his gun at the ready, he began to skirt the brush and circle below the three picketed horses.

Sweat beaded his brow and his lungs began to burn as he hurried below the cove and then climbed the next hill. By searching along the main trail below, he perceived the best cover for an ambush. Even as he continued his circumspection, he espied his cousin and Sergeant Fielding a short distance away, approaching via the main trail. From his higher position up the side of the incline, he determined the logical hiding places for the attack. The field of fire was a large open area, yet there was ample brush and rocky outcrops for cover.

He halted in mid-step, freezing in position as one of the ambushers raised his head up from his place of concealment. Knowing any movement might draw attention, Jared sank slowly down onto his knees. Then he crawled a few feet until he reached a taller stand of flora.

Panic set in. Fielding and Shane were almost at the clearing. He scrambled forward until he reached an opening in the trees and brush. A few steps took him to a higher mound on the hillside. He risked exposure, hoping the shooters would be watching their prey, and rose up to survey the landscape below. Time was running out!

CHAPTER NINE

Jared had seen where the first man was. A sweep of the terrain allowed him to spot the second, then a third. But his time was up. If there were more ambushers on horseback, he would have to draw their attention before they opened up on Shane and Fielding. Once he fired his first round, Shane and Fielding would instantly react and take cover. It wasn't exactly the way he had planned, but it gave them a fighting chance.

Throwing his gun to his shoulder, Jared used his hunting prowess. He adjusted his aim for the downward slope, the distance and the slight breeze – all within a single second – and chose the closest target.

The man was sighting down his own rifle, about to pull the trigger. . . .

An explosive blast from Jared's Winchester echoed through the canyon. The first attacker was struck in the chest by a well-placed round. He dropped like a watermelon rolling off of a cart.

The shot drew the attention of the two other shooters straightaway, both of them trying to locate Jared. Their reaction should have been to duck first, because Jared squeezed off another round.

A second ambusher staggered from his hiding place and collapsed to the ground. Even as Jared levered a third bullet into the chamber, the last man threw his gun down and raised his hands.

'Don't shoot!' he wailed. 'I give up!'

Jared searched both hillside and hollow, looking for any more attackers. Evidently, there were only three. He still maintained a vigil, gun ready, watching for any movement.

'Step out where I can get a look at you!' he hollered down. 'Anyone else pops up and I'll drop you like your two pals!'

The man walked out into the open and turned his head to look at the other two downed men. 'I'm all there is!' he shouted. 'There was just the three of us.'

Within a few minutes, Fielding and Shane had the surviving assailant bound with his hands behind his back, while Jared had retrieved and brought down both his and the bushwhackers' horses. They learned the names of the two dead men were Baldwin and Cooper. The last of the three was Olmstead.

'Now what?' Fielding asked, once they were all together. 'These three are enforcers up at Paradise, but that doesn't prove anything against Gaskell.'

Jared pointed his pistol at the remaining shooter. 'Tell us – who ordered this attack?'

Olmstead shook his head. 'I give you our names. It's all I'm going to give. Ain't nothing you can do about it.'

'He knows the money and power Gaskell has,' Fielding

said. 'Without proof of his involvement, we can't arrest Gaskell. With a good lawyer and a ton of money, this character might get off with a year or two behind bars.'

'A year or two!' Shane barked sharply. 'They were going to kill us dead and leave our bones to the buzzards!'

'I think we ought to make camp,' Jared suggested, leading the other two beyond Olmstead's hearing. 'We can have a bite to eat and decide how to proceed.'

Shane looked at him as if the toast had fell off his plate. 'Decide?' he said, shaking his head. 'What's to decide? These guys set up to kill us.'

'Olmstead looks like a reasonable guy,' Jared said, a twinkle in his eyes. 'I believe he will talk to us.'

Fielding scowled at Jared. 'There will be no torture of any prisoner while I'm around.'

'Trust me, Sergeant. I won't put a mark on him.'

The two men arrived in a rented carriage and were dressed in what the fashion conscious crowd called uptown suits and hats. They sought out Locke Valeron immediately and came to the front door of the main house.

Scarlet had been visiting her mother and the two of them summoned Locke. Cliff was working, and Mikki was in Nessy's room helping her with her schoolwork. Locke didn't invite the pair inside. He stepped out on the porch and closed the door to the house.

'State your business,' he directed.

'I am Percival Upshaw and this is my assistant,' the elder of the pair said importantly. 'I represent Mr Elmer Baddon and am serving your family with a summons. This request is sanctioned by the federal government, so the state has no say in the matter.'

Locke accepted the paper handed to him. 'A demand for us to produce Michelle Bruckner at a hearing in Denver,' he read the document. 'Three days?'

'That should be ample time for you to make the journey.' Upshaw sniffed impudently. 'And, I suggest you find yourself a lawyer to represent your side. The hearing will determine who has lawful guardianship of the child.'

'She's seventeen, not a child.'

'Nonetheless, you must appear before the court or a federal warrant will be issued for your arrest.'

Locke saw the judge's signature was not anyone he recognized. Obviously, Elmer had enough money and judicial clout to force him to produce the girl for the hearing.

'We'll be there,' he agreed.

'Fine. That's fine!' the attorney chirped, his chest puffed up like a river frog at dusk. 'I look forward to settling this expeditiously.'

'You've said your piece,' Locke told him bluntly. 'Now, get your money-grubbing can off of my property before I set the dogs on you both!'

Upshaw's eyes bugged and his face flushed pink. Without another word, he and his aide climbed aboard their buggy hastily and the rig left in a cloud of dust.

Wanetta and Scarlet came out to join Locke as the two men disappeared down the trail.

'We overheard the conversation,' Locke's wife said quietly. 'What options do we have?'

Locke looked at the paper again. 'This is a legal and

129

binding document. We will have to deliver Mikki to Denver for the hearing.'

'You said Baddon had money and power,' Scarlet spoke up. 'Is there anything our family can do?'

'Ask your husband to come see me,' Locke replied. 'I need him to ride in and send a telegraph message to Wendy and Wyatt. Then we'll decide who all is to make the trip.'

'Cliff won't stay behind,' Wanetta said. 'He has a vested interest in this — with or without thinking of Nessy's welfare.'

'Maybe Cliff could marry Mikki?' Scarlet tried another angle. 'If they were wed, Baddon would have no claim.'

'She isn't of age to wed without consent,' Wanetta nixed the idea. 'She would need permission from her guardian or parent. As it stands, Mr Baddon has the strongest claim to that position.'

Scarlet uttered a mild profanity. 'Yes, to be her guardian, but not to force her into marrying him! That's outrageous!'

'Money can buy most anything,' Locke ended the discussion. 'Have Landau see me as soon as possible. I'll write the message and have it ready for him.'

'Whatever you say, Father.'

Scarlet hurried away to her house, which was located a quarter-mile from the main courtyard. Wanetta waited until she was out of earshot before speaking again.

'What do we tell Mikki? This is going to break her heart.'

'Tell her we are going to the hearing to demand she be allowed to choose her guardian. We intend to fight for her freedom, no matter what the odds or cost.'

130

'Stand still, dummy!' Jared warned Olmstead. 'That piece of tree stump isn't all that solid.'

'You can't do this!' Olmstead wailed, balancing on a wooden block, his hands bound behind him and a noose around his neck. 'I have a right to a trial.'

'No one is taking away that right,' Jared assured him. 'I just need for you to pass this little test. You've heard of people who are unbalanced?'

'No, I ain't.'

'Well, it's a slang term for them what end up in lunatic asylums and such. It's to prove your cattle are all moving in the right direction… you know, that your brain is working the same as normal folks.'

'My leg is crampin' up!' the man whined. 'I don't know how long I can stay atop this here stump.'

'Better talk fast then, before you slip and hang yourself.'

'I ain't gonna hang myself. It's you who's trying to hang me!'

'Tsk, tsk, Olmstead,' Jared jeered at his complaint. 'You're starting to sound like a big baby, crying like that.'

'Where's Fielding?' he wanted to know. 'I demand you turn me over to him!'

'You demand?' Jared laughed derisively. 'You don't make demands, Olmstead. You tell me who sent you to kill us and I'll let loose the rope. After all, if you testify against Gaskell, the judge is bound to give you a lighter sentence.'

'Gaskell will never let this get to court. He'll get me out

of jail, just as soon as he learns you have me under arrest.'

'Why would he do that?' Jared asked. 'I mean, unless you were doing this on his orders.'

The man's lips pressed tightly together in stubborn rebellion. He was not going to be tricked into talking by some. . . .

A gun being fired caused Olmstead to jump, nearly falling from the thick stump. He twisted his head enough to see Jared had a smoking gun in his hand.

'What the hell are you doing?' he howled. 'I 'bout fell off.'

Jared displayed an impish grin. 'I just shot a chunk out of the wood you're standing on. You know, I'll bet I can collapse one side with one more slug. Whatta' yuh say? Should I give it another shot?'

He laughed. 'Get it? Give it another shot – for real!'

'Officer Fielding!' the man yelled at the top of his lungs. 'Come stop this crazy coot! He's gonna kill me!'

'How about I try to hit the notch right in the middle of that block of wood?' Jared continued to torment him. 'I'll bet you five bucks a perfect hit will split the log right in half. You game for a wager?'

'You're out of your mind!' Olmstead shouted. 'Why would I bet on something like that? I would die if it worked!'

'You're right,' Jared admitted. 'Why bet five dollars when you are already betting your life?' He grunted. 'Only one way to find out if you win or lose.' He snickered. 'Of course, to win the bet, you lose your life. Too bad . . . but those are the odds.'

He took careful aim and cocked his Colt. . . .

'No! Wait!' Olmstead shrieked. 'I'll tell you! I'll testify in court! I'll do whatever you say!'

Jared frowned. 'Don't be turning chicken on me. How are we going to know if a bullet will split that piece of wood if you cave like this?'

'Please! Call over Fielding! I'll tell him everything!'

Jared uttered a tiresome sigh. 'All right, but you're going to wonder about that next shot for the rest of your life.'

'At least I'll have a life,' Olmstead retorted. 'You crazy coot! You'd have hanged me on the spot.'

Being made aware of the hearing, Mikki couldn't hold back her tears. Cliff moved over and took her into his arms to console her. He held her like a child while she wept against his shoulder.

'I made you a sincere promise, Mikki,' he whispered next to her ear. 'Elmer will never touch you again. If I have to kill him, I'll keep that from happening.'

'No,' she murmured. 'I can't let you ruin your life. Nessy is so sweet. She needs you. You're the only family she can remember.'

'Dad knows a lot of powerful people; so does Wyatt and Brett. There's a whole passel of us to deal with only Baddon and his lawyers. If the judge rules in his favor, we'll go over his head to a higher court. If need be, we will keep this tied up in the courts until you are of legal age.'

Mikki leaned back. 'Why is your family doing this for me? Until I showed up on the doorstep, none of them had ever heard of me.'

'I told you about Nash Valeron, and how he and some

of the family took on the chore of saving Trina Barrett. He and Wendy didn't know her from a stray dog when she walked in their door. But they did what was right. People should always band together to fight injustice or crime. That goes double when the law can't or won't do what's right.'

The girl stared at him, her rich mahogany eyes still misted with tears, but a softness on her face like a mother holding her child for the first time.

'You're such a good man, Cliff,' she said. 'And this family… They are the salt of the earth.'

He reached up and brushed the tip of her nose. 'You're not exactly castor oil.'

She actually laughed. 'I have my faults.'

'Not in my eyes,' he said. 'Trust me when I say I've been looking for a girl like you all of my life. I didn't know it until you showed up at our dinner table, but I know it now.' He leaned forward and gently touched her lips with his own. Then added, 'And I'm not going to ever let you go.'

Wyatt and Wendy joined up with Shane and Jared. The four of them had dinner together and exchanged news.

Shane finished their tale by saying, 'Fielding had a heck of a time explaining to his captain about how come Olmstead was so forthcoming about Gaskell and the operation up at Paradise. All he could say was the two of us went to strap the two dead men over their horses, and when we returned, the enforcer from Paradise was singing like a meadowlark.'

'But you didn't touch him?' Wendy asked Jared.

'Nary a finger or hair on his head. I just tried to make a simple bet with him, and he folded like a greenhorn.'

'Well, all the news isn't good,' Wyatt silenced the levity. 'Baddon hired a big-time lawyer from St Louis. He served up some papers to Uncle Locke. They have to bring Mikki here to Denver for a court hearing.'

'The man has a lot of money,' Wendy said tightly. 'Why are men like Baddon and Gaskell the ones who have wealth and power? How come it isn't the good and righteous who prosper?'

'Remember what it says in the Bible about rich men,' Shane reminded them. 'Easier for a camel to pass through the eye of a needle than for a rich man to go to heaven.'

'Meaning we won't meet up with either of those fellows in the afterlife,' Wyatt said.

'I, for one, don't care to wait that long to end their reign here on earth,' Jared chimed in. 'Tomorrow, Fielding is taking a dozen men – along with me and Shane – and we're going to close down Paradise.'

'Yes,' Wendy said, 'but how do we protect Mikki?'

Wyatt answered. 'Locke will contact the governor's office and Brett can see what influence he can muster. I have to wonder if it will be enough.'

They discussed the situation for a time, but it was growing late. Soon the four of them were headed to the hotel.

Wyatt had a room to himself, as did Wendy. As for Shane and Jared, they had kept their room. Even as they entered the rooming house, Wendy took hold of Jared's hand.

'Dad wants me to find an attorney to defend Mikki in

the morning. I know you're going to be busy with this Paradise thing, but I need to talk to you for a minute,' she said quietly.

'Sure, sis. I'll walk you to your room.' He nodded to Shane. 'Be right up. Don't you start to snoring before I get there.'

Ronnie walked in on Gaskell to find Jane sitting on his lap! Seeing his friend's worried look, Gaskell stood up so quickly that she slipped off and landed hard in a sitting down position. She yelped from the sudden shock and then hurried to get to her feet. Before she could brush herself off, Gaskell gave her a shove toward the door.

'Get back to your desk!' he barked the order. 'No one comes in while Ronnie is in here with me.'

'OK, Ward,' she whimpered, rubbing her newly bruised backside. 'Whatever you say.'

As soon as she passed by Ronnie, he slammed the door shut. From his frantic expression, Gaskell knew things had not gone well.

'We're in it up to our chins, Ward,' Ronnie said breathlessly. 'Cooper and Baldwin are dead, and Olmstead was taken prisoner. He's singing like one of them opera gals at the top of his voice.'

'I don't believe it,' Gaskell growled. 'He knows I wouldn't let those inept lawmen put him in prison.'

'Donner had his ear at the window of the jail. Olm done told them how you ordered the attack on the two Valerons and Sergeant Fielding. He also blabbed about Adams – says he heard you give me the order to kill him and get rid of his body.'

'I'd forgotten he was the one who reported Adams missing.'

'Yep, he was standing not twenty feet away when you told me to deal with the runaway.'

'The yellow, lily-livered fool! He's ruined both of us!'

'The law and the Valerons will be headed this way at any minute. I think you ought to clean out your safe, take whatever money you can get your hands on, and let's skedaddle out of here.'

'Damn, Ronnie, I can't do that. I've got tens of thousands of dollars in the Denver bank. I can't just leave it behind.'

'I recollect hearing about something called restitution, Ward. They can take every dime you've got to pay all of the people they are going to set free from up here. From what Donner said, them law dogs intend to take every person under contract and return all of the prisoners for processing. That won't leave enough people to run a decent-sized chicken farm. We're out of business, pard. Plain and simple.'

Gaskell rubbed his temples while trying to conjure a plan. After a few moments, he put a hard look on Ronnie.

'We can still make a fight of it,' he said, his brain working quickly. 'We've got a dozen men who will join us.'

Ronnie shook his head. 'It's no good, Ward. They can bring the army up here. We can't fight the army!'

'No, we won't have to fight the army.'

'I'm listening, Ward.'

Gaskell got up and circled his desk. He was not accustomed to losing and he hated the idea of being closed down and possibly end up behind bars. After three empty trips around the room, he had a plan in mind.

'You're certain of the information? There will be a posse of sorts arriving in the next few hours to arrest us for murder?'

'Can't be no doubt.'

Gaskell doubled his fists. 'And you want to cut and run.'

'As fast as a couple horses can carry us.'

He slowly turned his head from side to side. 'I am inclined to agree with you. However, we need to get to the bank first. We can't leave all that money behind.'

'If you head for town, you'll run into the posse and they will arrest you on sight,' Ronnie surmised. 'And if we fight, there's a good chance we'll end up dead. Is a little money worth the price?'

'I'm talking about withdrawing a great deal of money – close to forty thousand dollars.'

'The bank doesn't have that kind of cash on hand,' Ronnie argued.

'No, but they can give us bank drafts that we can take to Wells Fargo. Then we can cash them at any Wells Fargo office in the country.'

'Yeah, but it's like I said: the law is between us and Denver. They are probably rounding up men as we speak.'

'That's why we are going to make a fight of it.'

'Ward, you ain't making a bit of sense. If we stand and fight, we're gonna lose.'

Gaskell grinned. 'Not if we capture the posse. We let them walk into a trap, then lock them up and make our getaway. They won't have thought to get a judge to freeze my personal bank account and won't be watching for us to show up in town. We will get the pay vouchers, then stop by a Wells Fargo office and deposit most of the money. Once we're out of this part of the country, we'll stop at every Wells Fargo station we come to and get as much cash as they have on hand. We should end up with enough to set us up for a good long time.'

'What about the boys? What do we promise them so they will stick with us?'

'Offer them a thousand dollars each. Once the posse is behind bars, we will head for Denver. Soon as they have their money, we will all split up in different directions. The law won't have a clue which way the two of us went.'

Ronnie laughed, although there was no humor in his eyes. 'You know I'm with you, Ward. If you say we stay and spring a trap, that's what we'll do.'

'Let them ride into town as if we know nothing,' Gaskell outlined. 'Capture as many as possible without any shooting, and tell the men to be damn sure not to kill any of the Valerons!' He swore. 'If one of them dies, we'll never be able to stop looking over our shoulders.'

'All right, Ward,' Ronnie acknowledged the orders. 'I'll have Drummer round up the enforcers and any of the others who will fight. Me, Shade and Donner will get them placed where they can do the most good. We'll salt their hides, throw the rest in jail, then grab our cayuses and be long gone before they manage to get free from their cells.'

'You tend to it personally. I'll gather what money I can from everything of value that I own. No need leaving any more behind than necessary.'

Ronnie smirked. 'Does that mean taking Jane along?'

Gaskell uttered a cruel chuckle. 'Her type is a dollar a bunch. We'll find plenty like her once we're set up.'

His friend laughed and made his exit.

Even as Ronnie hurried out the door, Gaskell was thinking of what he needed to pack for a quick getaway. First off, he would send Jane over to get Parker Sayles. The judge had a decision to make too. He wouldn't be any help in a fight, nor was he likely to be of any use in the future. However, he would give the man a chance to make up his own mind.

CHAPTER TEN

Locke and Cliff were the only ones to leave the ranch with Mikki. Nessy would be in Wanetta's care until they returned. Having wired ahead, Wendy had arranged for them to meet with a reputable attorney in Denver.

Cliff felt a fist close around his heart each time he looked at Mikki. Her eyes were red and swollen from crying, and he suspected she hadn't slept more than a few minutes at a time since learning of the hearing. Worse than watching her suffer, he hated the feeling of helplessness. He had promised her she would never have to see or be with Elmer again, yet the law was on the wealthy man's side. He knew Locke and the rest of the family would do everything they could, but the Valerons were honor bound to comply with the laws of the land.

The stage ride to Cheyenne had been made in silence, and then the train to Denver was an endless trek across the open expanse of countryside. Cliff did his best to lift the girl's spirits. He assured her that no marriage could be performed, not between a guardian and his ward, without her giving her consent. Plus, he vowed to stick by her side

141

as long as possible and never give up until she was free of Elmer's control. If it meant moving to Denver for the next couple of years, he was willing to do just that.

Rather than boost her bravado, the words sounded hollow and empty. Mikki remained taciturn and faced her future with a visible dread and morbid acceptance, like a man who, having watched the gallows being built, had decided to walk forward boldly and meet his fate.

Locke didn't make false promises, but he did offer moral support from time to time. He was friends with the governor; his family had worked with the Denver police several times; and Trina's ranch was only twenty miles from the city. He pointed out that the court would sometimes recognize a woman's independence at eighteen. That offered them a chance to make her stay with Elmer a term of only a few months.

All of their reinforcement did little for Mikki's state of mind. When the train pulled into the Denver station, she took hold of Cliff's hand and clung to his arm. She was no longer the spunky young woman who had entered the Valeron's household, but a frightened child fearful of what lay ahead.

Wendy was there to meet them. She hugged her father then flung her arms around Mikki's neck. She gave her a warm hug and whispered a few words of encouragement into her ear.

Cliff did not hear what was said, but Mikki stared back at Wendy with a perplexed mien. It was an odd look, unfathomable to him, but a glimmer of light seemed to return to her usually sparkling eyes.

'I have two beds in my room,' Wendy informed her

father. 'I spoke to the hotel owner and he allowed that you and Cliff could sleep in Shane and Jerry's room. They aren't expected to get back until sometime tomorrow.'

'Where have they gone?' Locke wanted to know.

'Wyatt and the law are with them, all headed to Paradise. They have a lot of work to do up there. If they should return before morning, Wyatt has a room and the boys can get another.'

'Let's put our luggage away and you can fill us in on what all is going on. What time is the hearing?'

'Tomorrow afternoon. I'm hoping everything will be wrapped up so we can catch the train back to Cheyenne day after tomorrow morning. I'm anxious to get back. Martin helped July with the monthly report or our businesses, but my birthday party is only a few days away.'

'Ah, yes,' Locke said with a smile. 'My baby girl's birthday. There's a date I will never forget.'

Cliff and Locke went to the assigned room while Wendy took Mikki with her. They would freshen up and then meet for a meal a bit later.

'I have to tell you, Uncle,' Cliff said, once they had entered their hotel room. 'I can't stand by and allow Elmer to take Mikki away. She is terrified of being with him. That filthy maggot mistreated her before; I can't let him hurt her again.'

'Trust me, Cliff,' Locke replied in a cool voice. 'We are here to see the man never harms Mikki again.'

'But what if the judge rules in Elmer's favor?'

'We will take it to a higher court.'

Cliff sighed deeply. 'Sometimes I wish I could return to the callous, carefree louse I used to be. This worrying about a woman is eating me up inside.'

'Perhaps God is giving you a little of your own medicine. You did dirt to a great many girls before you adopted Nessy. This could be poetic punishment.'

'There isn't anything poetic about it,' Cliff lamented. 'He's made me completely miserable.'

Jared had been riding point. He appeared on the trail to stop the small force that was headed for Paradise.

'Got someone coming down the trail,' he told Fielding, him being in charge of the posse. 'It's a man, a woman, and two kids.'

Fielding tipped his head at Munson. 'The rest of you get off the road. Jared and I will check this family out, but we don't want anyone seeing the size of our party just yet.'

Munson, Wyatt, Shane and the group of police officers quickly moved off into the nearby trees. They had reached cover before the wagon appeared on the trail.

Fielding stopped the family with a raised hand and greeting smile. Before he had a chance to speak, Officer Munson came riding over to stop at his side.

'It's Benny Janks,' he informed Jared and Fielding. 'He's the mine foreman from Paradise.'

Janks gave him a crooked look. 'So you ain't studying to be no mine inspector.' He harrumphed. 'I thought you seemed a mite skittish for someone trying to learn the ins and outs of mining. That Faro character fooled me; he seemed genuine.'

'He's my cousin,' Jared told him. 'He runs both of our mines up at the Valeron ranch.'

Janks bobbed his head. 'Seemed a nice fella.'

144

'Where are you going with the family?' Fielding asked. 'The carryall you're driving has a lot of belongs stacked on it.'

'I quit my job,' he said. 'Hated to leave the big money and position, but them boys are gearing up for a battle. I ain't about to risk my family in a war against the law.'

'What makes you think there's a war coming?' Fielding wanted to know.

'I ain't blind, Mr Lawman. Gaskell's partner from Denver arrived a few hours ago with his two sidekicks. Now every man-jack who carries a gun is loading up for a military action. I told Drummer I was leaving and didn't even stick around to claim my pay. A few dollars ain't worth getting me or one of my family kilt.'

'We're always hiring good men,' Jared said. 'I reckon Faro could use a man with your experience to help oversee our two mines. It's a lot of work for him to manage both of them, especially due to the mines being a day's ride apart.'

'Wyoming is a long way to go without being sure of a job,' Janks replied.

'Faro said you knew your stuff,' Jared praised. 'He'll give you a job and, although the single men stay in bunkhouses, we provide cottage-style, two-bedroom houses for the married men.'

'I'm beholden to you, Mr Valeron.'

Jared gave a negative shake of his head. 'I'm sure you'll earn your keep.'

'One question, if I might,' Fielding spoke up. 'Do you know how many men Gaskell is going to have against us?'

'Didn't look like more than ten to a dozen,' Janks said.

145

Then, meaningfully, 'But the way they were sneaking about, I suspect they're going to invite you to waltz right up the main street.'

'Thanks,' Fielding said. 'I hope you do well at the Valeron spread. I'm told they hire only the best, so I figure you will fit right in.'

The man lifted a hand in farewell and continued down the road. Both of his kids waved.

Wyatt and the others came out to join them. 'Heard some of that,' he said. 'I recall seeing the man when I was in Paradise.'

'He said Gaskell is getting ready for us,' Jared advised him. 'Going to leave the front door open and close it when we step through.'

Wyatt displayed a sly simper. 'Maybe a few of us should try the back way?'

'My thought exactly, cuz,' Jared announced. 'You, me and Shane can circle down below the town and slip in unseen. With any luck, we can toss a juicy-ripe road apple into the cake they've baked for their little surprise party.'

'Be dark in a couple hours,' Fielding contributed. 'We would make harder targets without the brightness of the sun.'

'And it would give us time to infiltrate their rear defenses,' Wyatt went with the idea.

'That's the plan, then,' Fielding proposed. 'I had hoped they would allow us to ride in and discuss the options – prior to arresting a couple of them – but the hand has been dealt.'

'We'll look forward to seeing you about dusk,' Wyatt said. 'Stay clear of any shootouts till we give you a signal.'

Fielding grinned. 'I'm sure we will recognize the signal.'

The family, other than Mikki – who didn't feel like eating – met up with the attorney over the evening meal. Wendy introduced Burton Lloyd and they sat together at a corner table of the restaurant. Locke led the conversation, but the lawyer offered little promise. After some back and forth notions and suggestions, Lloyd sighed his resignation.

'I wish I could be more optimistic, Mr Valeron, but this seems a long shot at best. Without proof that Elmer actually harmed the young lady while in his care, we have no case. He took Miss Bruckner in and acted as her guardian for seven years. That is going to be hard to contest.'

'What about intending to marry the child you helped raise?' Wendy exploded. 'What kind of lowlife miscreant would do something like that? It's disgusting and immoral!'

'I agree,' he concurred. 'But it won't be allowed in evidence, because he hasn't yet filed for a marriage license. That means we can only deal with the topic of guardianship.'

'He got another girl pregnant,' Locke was outstandingly blunt. 'The poor young thing ended her own life rather than suffer the shame of giving birth to a fatherless child. The man is responsible for both of their deaths!'

The lawyer did not waver. 'It isn't pertinent to the guardianship, Mr Valeron. He denied that the child was his.' The man did not hide his dismay. 'Believe me, I've gone over the law books and searched for hours on end.

There is nothing about this custody hearing that works in our favor. Without proof of Mr Baddon's abuse, and no way to establish he was responsible for Miss Lopez's condition, I can see no way to stop him from reclaiming control of the girl.'

'I'll expect you to do your best for us all the same,' Locke told Lloyd.

'Yes, sir. I'll give the judge every argument I can think of, including asking to have Mikki put on the stand. She can attest to your need for a nanny and living with an upstanding family. That works in our favor because Mr Baddon had hired her out as a nanny for several years. I'll also insist she is old enough to decide for herself who she wants to live with. Trust me, I'll throw everything I can at the judge. But,' he warned, 'even if we get this judge to let you have Miss Bruckner, a higher court can overrule his verdict. We have no lawful foundation for a ruling in our favor. I'm sorry, but that is how our judicial system works.'

Locke, Wendy and Cliff left the restaurant with heavy hearts. They knew the chance of winning Mikki's freedom was next to nil.

'I'm not going to tell Mikki what the lawyer said,' Wendy told Cliff and her father. 'She needs all of her courage to face this ordeal.'

'You're right, daughter,' Locke concurred. 'It will be difficult enough for her to go through the process. I regret there isn't anything we can do.'

'I feel completely powerless,' Cliff said. 'If this was an ordinary guy, we could buy him off. But he has money and can't be bought.'

'Can't really threaten him either,' Locke put in. 'He is

able to hire a dozen gunmen to throw against us. Plus, he will have the law on his side.'

Wendy stopped at the hotel lobby, rose up onto her toes and kissed Locke on the cheek. 'We are doing all we can, Daddy. I'm proud of you for being here.'

Locke and Cliff watched her turn and go up the stairs to her room.

'I'm not a drinking man,' Locke said to Cliff. 'But I'll buy you a glass of wine.'

'If you don't mind, Uncle, I'd prefer a beer.'

The three Valerons reached the west entrance to Paradise as the sun was setting. It helped their approach because the final rays of sun would be in the eyes of anyone watching the back road into town.

'I see one of them!' Shane whispered excitedly. 'There, on the roof of the livery.'

Wyatt had his field glasses out, making a slow sweep of the area. 'He's the only one, Jer.'

'They didn't expect anyone to come in the back way,' Jared guessed.

'The guard chose a good position,' Wyatt pointed out. 'He's got a rifle and is a good fifteen feet off of the ground.'

'How can we get to him?' Shane wondered aloud. 'If we try climbing up on the roof, he and anyone else watching is bound to see us.'

'Ye of little faith,' Jared said. Then he dug through his saddle-bags and pulled out a slingshot.

'You gotta be kidding?' Shane cried. 'When is the last time you used that?'

'A week or so ago. You know those pesky crows that keep getting into Aunt Gwen's garden? I've taken out a dozen or more of them in the last month or so.'

'Why use the slingshot on birds?' Wyatt wondered. 'Why not shoot them?'

'Best time to get a crow is early morning or about dusk. They don't pick up the flight of the rock that way. And Gwen gets riled if I fire a gun close to her house. You know the fuss she makes about frivolous shooting.'

Wyatt looked at the man sitting on the barn roof and frowned. 'You could always best me with a sling when we were kids. But trying to hit him so he doesn't cry out? That's going to take some luck.'

'Not if I get close enough. The tool shed is only a short way from the barn. It's not quite as high, but I won't be more than fifty feet away. Most of the crows I've taken out were at least that far . . . and if you don't hit them in the head, they simply fly off.'

'We'll get our guns and follow after you,' Wyatt told him. 'If you miss, we'll have to start our attack from the rear when he sounds the alarm.'

Jared moved with a hunter's stealth, closing the distance quickly via an indirect route around a corral full of horses. He had a natural way of calming the animals and got by without them setting up a ruckus. He didn't trust to rocks, but always carried a small bag of steel balls, about the size of acorns. They were much more accurate than using something that had various weights, sizes and shapes.

Once to the shed, he studied the area, making a quick visual sweep for anyone who might see him climb atop the building. When satisfied it was safe, he scaled the structure, rose up onto his knees, took quick aim and let go the steel ball.

The shot was not perfect, though he scored a hit near the top of the sentry's skull. The ricochet knocked off his hat, but stunned him enough that he fell over backwards and slid off of the roof. Fortunately, it made little sound... other than a 'thud' as he hit the ground.

Shane was on him before the guard knew he had been knocked from his perch. He had him bound and gagged within seconds.

'Good shooting,' Wyatt praised Jared's shot.

'Easier than hitting a crow, cuz,' Jared bragged.

'I'll never doubt your prowess with a slingshot again,' Shane added with a chortle. 'You're probably an expert marksman with an Indian lance too.'

Jared grunted. 'They are too cumbersome to carry around in my saddle-bags.'

Wyatt outlined the next step. 'I figure each of us can seek out one of the gang. We take him out quietly, if possible, and then get set before giving the signal for the attack. A frontal assault by Fielding should allow us to find the others and put them out of commission right quick.'

'Yeah,' Shane grumbled. 'But how do we keep from getting shot by Fielding and his men by accident?'

'Keep your head down,' both Wyatt and Jared said in unison.

Gaskell heard the shooting, but it was short and sporadic, as if there hadn't been much of a fight. He hoped that meant the trap had worked. Everything was packed into a pair of saddle-bags, ready to go. All he needed now was to see the lawmen and Valerons being herded to the jail. Without help or a key, it should take them a full day to break out. Come morning, he and his men would leave for Denver an hour before daylight. They would be there when the bank opened and clean out his account. He could get vouchers for his men, so as to give him as much cash as possible. Then he and Ronnie would separate from the rest of their men, with everyone to manage their own escape. Parker had opted not to leave Paradise, afraid he would look guilty of being more than Gaskell's lawyer. He didn't favor life on the run, even if paid well.

Suddenly, Ronnie came scrambling into the room. His eyes were wide with alarm, gun in his hand, and missing his hat. He slammed the door shut behind him and grabbed hold of Gaskell's arm.

'Come on, Ward!' he cried. 'Things are out of control! We've lost the fight!'

'What?' Gaskell howled. 'But how did. . . .'

'They got in behind us. When the lawmen appeared at the edge of town, half of our men had already been taken out by the Valerons. We're done!'

'How the . . .'

But Ronnie cut him off. 'All of the men have tossed their guns! I barely managed to slip away. Shade and Drummer – Donner – the rest of them have all been captured.'

Before Gaskell could pick up his saddlebags from the desk, they heard footsteps from the next room. Jane screamed and they could hear her being escorted out of the building.

'Come out with your hands up!' a voice commanded a moment later. 'This is the law!'

Gaskell grit his teeth, filled with loathing and rage. His well-laid plans were dust. There would be no escape, no grabbing the money at the bank and starting anew. His private world had been invaded and destroyed.

Ronnie was still breathing hard, but he showed no cowardice. 'They'll hang us both, Ward,' he said, his teeth clenched and a hard set to his eyes. 'I'm not gonna dance at the end of a rope.'

Gaskell swallowed a gulp of reality. He slowly pulled his gun and gave his lifelong friend a final look. 'Nor me either, pard.'

Ronnie, his gun in his fist, took hold of the doorknob. 'We're comin' out!' He shouted. 'Prepare to die!'

The door was thrown wide, he and Gaskell charged forward . . .

A volley of gunfire filled the air!

Wyatt and Fielding stood over the two bodies. Both men had gone down in the hail of bullets, neither getting off a decent shot of their own.

'Guess there will be no trial for these two,' Fielding said.

'The lawyer, Sayles, he said the bank holds the deed to the mine and some of the holdings. They will have to figure a way to get this place back into operation.'

'Without the prisoners and contracted workers, they are going to need to hire about a hundred people.'

Wyatt added: 'I'm sure many of those living here will stick around for a while. After all, the wages will be pretty good so long as the mine continues to turn out high-grade ore.'

Shane entered the room wearing a wide grin. 'Not a single one of our men was injured in the shoot-out.'

'Because you Valerons took out most of the opposition,' Fielding extolled the plan. 'Most of the resistance had their hands lifted before we entered town.'

'We got lucky,' Wyatt admitted.

Fielding looked around. 'Where's Jared?'

'The lookout we took out first worked himself free,' Shane informed them sheepishly. 'Jerry grabbed up his horse and went after him.'

'Pretty sloppy job with a full length of rope,' Wyatt said, looking at Shane. 'Gonna have to put you on the branding crew so you can learn to tie someone off properly.'

'Hey, we were in a hurry!' Shane protested. 'Besides which, he looked like his lights would be out all night long. Jer hit him pretty good with that steel ball.'

'Well,' Fielding took charge, 'let's get the enforcers and other gunmen locked away for the night. We will take turns on guard – at least two men on watch at all times – then head for town after we sort out the prison laborers tomorrow. A good many of the convicts will likely get an early release, so I doubt we'll have any trouble with them.'

'And the contracted employees?' Shane wanted to know.

'They can stay on for wages for the time being. Once the bank appoints someone to oversee the holdings, they will have the option of working here or moving on.'

'Sounds like you've got everything figured out,' Wyatt praised Fielding.

'Yeah, well, I'll leave Officer Munson to work with Parker Sayles. The two of them can watch over the place until the bank takes over. That will keep any of the rest of us from having to stick around.'

'I hope Jer doesn't get lost in the dark,' Shane said. 'I know he's the best tracker in the country, but it's going on to full dark.'

'He'll probably be back by the time we pull out . . .' Wyatt opined, 'Or he will meet us in Denver. Jerry knows what he's doing.'

CHAPTER ELEVEN

Other than the Valeron group, only the required people attended the hearing for Mikki's guardianship: the judge, a clerk, a deputy marshal and the two attorneys for Elmer Baddon. As the time for the hearing approached, Elmer did not yet put in an appearance. Finally, the judge pulled out his pocket watch and stared at the pair of out-of-town, extremely expensive lawyers.

'Do you expect Mr Baddon directly?' the magistrate asked. 'I don't look with favor on those who keep the court waiting.'

'I don't know where he can be,' the lead attorney said. 'We conferred with Mr Baddon over dinner last night. He seemed most anxious to get this over with. I can't imagine . . .'

He paused as the door to the courtroom opened. It was not Elmer, however, but one of the city policemen. He carried a wrinkled sheet of paper in his hand.

'If you'll pardon the interruption, Your Honor,' the lawman said. 'I have something you should see.'

He gestured the man to come forward, listened to him

as he spoke in a hushed voice, then accepted the parchment. When he looked at it, his mouth fell open in shock.

'What do you know of this?' he demanded of the policeman.

'There have been rumors about Mr Baddon, but no one has ever produced enough proof to charge him with a crime.'

Mikki's attorney patted her arm in a show of support and rose to his feet. 'Your Honor,' Lloyd asked, 'might I inquire as to if this interruption is related to our case?'

The judge gave an affirmative nod. 'I believe this note and new information will have a direct bearing on the current issue before the court.'

Everyone in the room waited in such silence one might have heard the sneeze of a gnat. Then the magistrate held up the paper. 'This message reads: *I am a child molester and was responsible for the deaths of Gina Lopez and her unborn child.*

The judge laid the note aside and addressed the lawman. 'State for the court where you found this note?'

'It was pinned to the chest of Elmer Baddon,' the policeman declared. 'He was found hanging from a tree not a hundred yards from his house.'

'Have you begun the hunt for his killer?'

'We searched all around the area but couldn't find a scrap of evidence. Near as we could tell, it appears as if Mr Baddon hung himself. We didn't find a single track of anyone else, and the fancy braided rope was from one of the window drapes in his house.'

'I trust your department will do a thorough investigation,' the judge said.

'Yes, sir, Your Honor. A couple of the men are still at the scene.'

Turning to the case in hand, the man wearing the black robe raised his gavel. 'Pursuant with this tragic event, the guardianship of Mikki Bruckner is hereby granted to Locke and Wanetta Valeron. They shall have custody of her until the age of twenty-one or at such time as she should wed.' He brought down the gavel. 'This court is adjourned.'

Mikki threw her arms around Locke's neck, then turned to Cliff and did the same. She was ecstatic, practically bubbling over with the thrill of the court decision and being free of the clutches of Elmer Baddon.

'How about that?' Locke spoke to Wendy. 'Perhaps the man was afraid Mikki would tell the truth about him?'

'Could be,' Wendy replied. 'The filthy, debauched vermin has been molesting children for years. Even if there wasn't any proof, everyone would know his dirty secret.'

'As the girl, Gina Lopez, died at sixteen and was with child, that would support any charge Mikki might have made,' Cliff agreed. 'The guy should have been drawn and quartered back when she died!'

'Most importantly,' Wendy said, 'He will never hurt a child ever again.'

Locke displayed gratification. 'You're right, my very charming daughter. Justice for his heinous crimes took too long coming, but it is done.' Then with a narrow look, 'And it's a relief to know Jared was twenty miles away, up at Paradise. I'll bet he has an ironclad alibi.'

Wendy displayed complete naivety. 'It's an obvious suicide, Daddy. Jerry doesn't need an alibi. Besides which, he has been working with Brett, Shane and Wyatt. They are all working with the police to eliminating the indentures and crimes at the town of Paradise. There's no way he could have been involved in this.'

'Just an observation, daughter,' Locke replied. Then on to another subject. 'Can we still expect an announcement at your party?'

'Only if you get me home in time to have the party.'

'Riders coming in,' Cliff called from the courthouse doorway. 'Looks like Jer, Shane and Wyatt are all in one piece. Them and the lawmen have a small army of prisoners and other people in tow.'

'Let's go greet them, Daddy,' Wendy chirped gleefully. 'We've got great news to tell them about Mikki!'

'I'm sure it will come as a great relief to all of the boys,' Locke said.

As the small cavalcade approached, Jared, Shane and Wyatt broke off from the others. The prisoner next to Fielding could be overheard complaining about his head.

'I tell yuh, I don't 'member a thing. I can't figure how I got so far into the hills, not after being hit in the head by that there steel ball.'

'It doesn't matter now,' Fielding replied back. 'Valeron run you to ground and you're going to jail along with the rest of Gaskell's toughs.'

'I sure don't feel tough no more,' he whined. 'My head is killing me.'

'Welcome back, boys!' Locke greeted them. 'Looks like everything turned out fine.'

'Fielding has a lot of sorting to do with all of the prisoners who were working at Paradise,' Wyatt spoke up. 'Not to mention, we've eight men in custody who are facing charges.'

'Gaskell took the easy way out,' Shane added. 'Him and a few of his henchmen died fighting.'

'How about the hearing?' Jared wanted to know.

'Yeah,' Wyatt joined in. 'I see the nanny is with you. Did you win the case or get some kind of extension?'

'Elmer Baddon apparently hanged himself last night,' Cliff told them. 'He stuck a note to his shirt admitting to being a child molester and being responsible for the death of a young girl and her unborn child.'

'The hell you say!' Wyatt declared. 'Durned if that don't save me the trouble of killing him.'

'You would have had to stand in line behind me,' Jared avowed. 'I was looking forward to feeding that child abuser a few ounces of lead.'

Cliff put his arm around Mikki's shoulders. 'See what I told you?' he said. 'We Valerons are men of our words. Ain't no way Elmer was ever going to get his grubby hands on you again.'

Mikki laughed happily. 'I'll never doubt your word again, Clifford.'

'Enough of this mundane chatter,' Wendy spoke up. 'We've got a train to catch. Now that everything is copacetic, I don't intend to miss my own birthday party!'